Murder Without a Duck

A Simpato Mystery

CLAUDIA H. LONG

Sibylline Press

Copyright @ 2024 by Claudia H. Long

All Rights Reserved. Published in the United States
by Sibylline Press, an imprint of All Things Book LLC,
California. Sibylline Press is dedicated to publishing
the brilliant work of women authors ages 50 and older.
www.sibyllinepress.com

Sibylline Press
Paperback ISBN: 9781960573377
eBook ISBN: 9781960573254
Library of Congress Control Number: 2024949057

Cover Design: Alicia Feltman

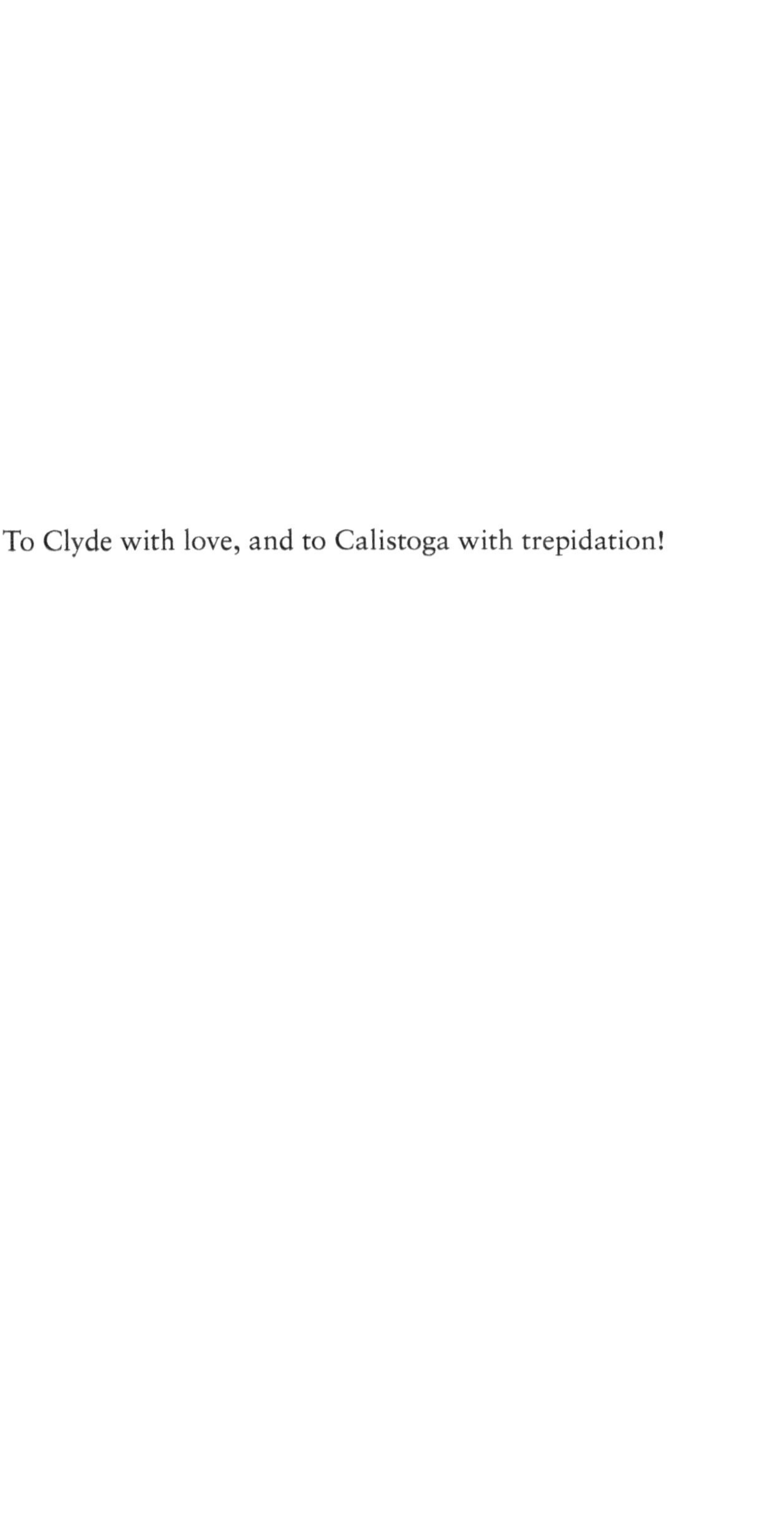

To Clyde with love, and to Calistoga with trepidation!

From BackQuack

A look back at Simpato's history, from long ago and not so long ago

We always say that nothing bad ever happens in Simpato. But history proves us otherwise.

Ten years ago, Simpato was rocked by the shocking discovery of the body of a local real estate developer under the bridge over the Valley River. He had drowned in the heavy rains of that December, leaving his son devastated by the loss. The development he was about to break ground on died with him.

Not three months later, our quiet town was again struck with tragedy when our beloved Keeper and her husband were lost at sea while on a sailing voyage to Hawai'i. The secrets she kept for us were sunk in the briny deep.

In a town as peaceful as Simpato, these losses remain scars of grief on the psyche of the populace. Much healing has taken place since then, but our little world will never be the same.

CHAPTER ONE

An eardrum-cracking horn blasted from a black pickup truck at the end of my new driveway. The window rolled down, and a young man raised a beer can to me. "Welcome to the neighborhood, Keeper!" A second blast, followed by four bars of "Never on Sunday" in brass notes, reverberated as he tire-squealed past the movers' truck now backing out of the drive. The movers grinned, and one saluted me as they made the turn onto the main road.

What have I done?

★ ★ ★

I thought I'd made only one big mistake in my life—or maybe two. Marrying Saul DeVine was definitely the first mistake, and listening to him was the second. Without one there wouldn't be the other, so maybe I could count the second as part of the first and keep the score low.

The divorce, on the other hand, hadn't been a mistake. Neither was the generous marital settlement. Saul knew my silence had a steep price, and he gladly paid it. Of course, he could afford it. That's what got us into trouble in the first place.

But moving into my parents' old summer home in Simpato, California, may have been the third mistake. I was just beginning to find out, and I hadn't even finished unpacking yet.

I pushed at the last of the boxes the movers had delivered. The boxes sat in the middle of the living room because the house had exactly four rooms: living/dining room, bedroom, bathroom, and kitchen. Nine hundred square feet of what the realtors called "cozy" living space, set on a half-acre of absolutely prime downtown real estate, and all mine—even if the actual title to the house wasn't *all* in my name.

The house had been my parents'—of blessed memory— summer cottage, and it was still in their name, along with mine. Deferred maintenance didn't begin to describe the condition of the house; it had been vacant for nearly a decade. Even so, I had definitely breathed a sigh of major relief when I packed up my sleek condo in San Francisco and headed up the valley to the charming town of Simpato. Alone.

I pulled the step stool over to the bookcase. Step stools were a big part of my life. I reached up, putting the few law books I still owned up on the top shelf. They didn't need to be handy. For one thing, whatever I wanted to research was online now, and no one used actual paper books to look anything up. For another, I was disbarred.

You're not actually disbarred, I reminded myself. Just suspended for sixty days. Starting yesterday. Before I could start perseverating on the whole story, or deteriorating into a puddle of fury and humiliation, I pulled the law books off the shelf and threw them back in the box. I'd have to rent a unit at the storage facility I'd noticed a mile out of town, where they could molder for the two months of my suspension, along with anything else that didn't fit into my new, cozy space.

Once the rest of the non-law books were unpacked and shelved, I folded the remaining empty boxes. I put the ones with things that didn't belong in my new life on the back deck, ready for their trip to storage. I was surprised, after my ruthless paring down of the things I would bring, that I still had three full boxes of items, along with a large chair that would have to live in storage due to its size alone.

I mopped my face, spreading sweat and dust across my cheekbones, and flopped down into the other chair, the one that was staying. Home. And a new life. And now, to figure out how to live it.

At least I'd made this newest of possible mistakes by myself, rather than just being in the same life with my finally ex-husband. I would survive.

The first order of survival was food. That meant a trip to the Simpato grocery store, known as the Duck Shop. The duck theme was prevalent here in Simpato, thanks to the town's nickname. Though it made its presence known on the map as Simpato, everyone called it Sin-Pato, Spanish for *Without a Duck*. So of course they called the grocery store the Duck Shop. Lake Simpato—a weedy, green pond of a place most of the year—was the No-Duck Lake or the Duckless Pond. And the local weekly newspaper was the *Quack*. God only knew what they called the medical center.

I pulled myself off the chair, brushing white cat hair off my black yoga pants. "Damn cat," I muttered, not meaning it. I missed Luna, but Saul had kept her, either to impress his intern-turned-girlfriend—yes, another delightful fact in our divorce—or as a bargaining chip. While he no doubt regretted keeping the cat already, I'd still have to negotiate to get Luna back. Meanwhile, white fur remained a souvenir on everything, especially on black yoga pants.

I checked my look in the full-length mirror propped up against the bathroom wall. Hanging the mirror would keep till tomorrow. It would have been nice to be tall, like my mother; or blond like my father; or even fashionably curvy like my sister, but I was short, thin, with straight brown hair showing its first threads of gray among the red highlights. I dragged my hair into a ponytail and looked closely at my face. Not only did it need washing, on a serious level, but some moisturizer would go a long way, too. I settled for water. Soap was on the shopping list.

★ ★ ★

I pulled into a space in the Duck Shop parking lot, noting that I was one of the few non-pickups and fewer non-BMWs in the lot. My Prius, modest and fuel-efficient, gave a vaguely self-righteous sigh as I shut the driver's side door. The Duck Shop was only four blocks from my new home, but I knew that lugging five or six bags of groceries, even on a balmy April day, was not in the cards. The Prius didn't approve of short runs like this and clearly disliked the company it was being forced to keep.

"Lump it," I said.

"Sorry?"

I whirled. A woman dressed entirely in white was standing far closer than appropriate and uncomfortably so for me, since I couldn't move past her. The woman's pickup was parked on the line, facing out instead of head-in, and barely gave me enough room to squeeze between the cars—even without the human blockade.

"Huh?" I said, going for innocence.

"Did you just tell me to lump it, after you touched my truck?" The woman towered over me, but then, most people did.

"I was talking to my car," I said.

The woman peered down at me. "Really? You do too?"

"Yup. And my car has an attitude, so I have to keep it in line."

"Oh my god! So does my truck! And I was about to tell you, it's perfectly okay to tell my truck to lump it. Carinna," she added, holding out her hand. "Also known as the White Lady. Which is less than convenient these days."

"Sal. Nice to meet you."

"You new here? I haven't seen you around."

There are about eight thousand people in Simpato, so that seemed a little extreme but, since it was true, I copped to it. "Just finished moving in today. Hitting the Duck for some groceries."

"Well, you already seem to know the lingo," Carinna said.

"My parents owned a house here," I said. Why was I telling a complete stranger this? "I'm living in it now."

"Oh! So you're the new Keeper."

"Keeper?" I flashed on the black pickup and its driver's words.

"You know, Keeper of the House of Secrets?" I shook my head. "Are you sure you aren't?"

I shifted away a bit, still wedged between the two vehicles, blocked by the White Lady. "No clue. But off to get my groceries," I tried, turning sideways and hoping to slide.

"You living in the little blue house with the big yard on Second Street?" I nodded gingerly. "'House of Secrets,' it's called. I knew your parents. Lovely people. Hippies, very cool. I'd guess they would have told you about the Secrets."

I have no idea what this lunatic is talking about, I thought. Again, I shook my head.

"You *do* know that folks used to visit your mother, years and years ago? And would tell your mom everything?" Her sentences all ended in a question. I kept shaking my head. She went on. "And I mean *everything*. Your mother was the Keeper. I guess you are, now? Well, got to go. Can't spend the whole day chatting, not like some people."

Carinna reached for the pickup truck's door, forcing me to back up further. The pickup's door swung wide, smacking the Prius's mirror. "Lump it!" Carinna said gaily, and hopped into her truck. "Catch you around!

★ ★ ★

I picked up a copy of the *Quack* at the checkout stand and tossed it on top of the scouring cleanser, soap, window cleaning fluid, a pile of vegetables, and a pack of a dozen chicken thighs.

"Those vegetables are gonna rot before you eat them all, just you," the checker said.

"Excuse me?"

"You're the new Keeper, aren't you? And since it's just you, how are you going to eat all these veggies before they go bad?"

"I'll make soup," I answered.

This was not normal.

"Suit yourself," the checker said. "Slide your card, the chip don't work."

★ ★ ★

The Prius absorbed the bags of groceries and sundries without complaint. I pulled out and drove the few blocks back to my house and was turning into the driveway when a blast of a horn made me slam on my brakes. The Prius squealed angrily. I looked behind me, and that black pickup filled my rearview mirror again. I inched forward, turned into the drive, and stopped.

The same man leaned across the truck's interior to the open passenger window and waved his cap at me, then burned rubber roaring down Second Street. At the corner, he backfired before taking the turn.

What the hell?

I lugged my groceries up the rear steps, past the chair and the boxes, and let myself in through the back door, straight into the kitchen. It wasn't unfamiliar. After all, my parents had spent summers here for twenty years. But I'd never heard this business about the Keeper. My folks hadn't ever mentioned it. Then again, they only came for the summer. The rest of the year they lived in Sacramento, but summers there were unbearable, while Simpato had the benefit of a residue of coastal coolness, with less fog.

I also hadn't noticed the loud trucks and the intimacy of the small town when I visited.

I guess I should make soup, I thought, putting away the food. A good chicken and vegetable, with noodles, would be nutritious and restorative.

★ ★ ★

My groceries unloaded, the house more or less clean, and chicken soup simmering on the stove, I threw myself on the bed. The next thing I knew, the sun was slanting through the windows, and I had absolutely no clue where I was. In San Francisco, my old bedroom got morning light, not evening. Something else to get used to.

I couldn't get too lost since the bathroom was the next door over, but the smell of scorching chicken soup made the kitchen the first stop. Once the stove was off and immediate needs were taken care of, I looked at the mess in the pot. Salvageable? Like my life, only if I scraped gingerly from the top, never going too deep.

I set myself a plate on the little table in the corner of the living room closest to the kitchen, and sat down to my heavily metaphorical now-stew and a glass of the local wine. The main industry of Simpato was viticulture, a fancy word for grape-growing, with wineries and hospitality a close second. Three-quarters of the wine sold at the Duck Shop was made locally, and I would bet that the cashier would give you one hairy eyeball if you bought nonlocal.

I opened the *Quack* to read as I ate. The high-school band was having a concert; the senior center was having a crafts show; the mayor was being lambasted in a few letters to the editor; and there would be an additional green trash pickup next week. All in a week's work for a small town.

This week's BackQuack column, with historical tidbits on Simpato's past, featured the silver mines on Mount Santabella. Santabella loomed over the back of Simpato, its lower levels terraced to vineyards, its upper reaches craggy and treeless. It had been a volcano in its best days, and the ash and lava had created the spectacularly fertile soil of the world-famous valley of which Simpato was the very, very most distant tip. From my house I could see the upper portion of the mountain, dotted with dark spots where silver was once mined.

BackQuack reminded us that silver was the first draw for Spanish settlers, bent on Christianizing or exterminating the prosperous and peaceful Native inhabitants of the valley. Mine tours, offered by the Valley historical society and led by the librarian, were available on the first Saturday of every month, weather permitting.

On the next page, featuring a large pen-and-ink drawing of a nose, was the feature entitled "Georgiana Knows!" The *Quack* had its own gossip columnist, someone named Georgiana, and the column, referred to as The Nose, was mercifully not called anything duck-related. Though the items, such as they were, contained some bad duck puns, like everything else in this town.

> *Seen waddling down Main Street, a downy group of ducklings, all in their Brownie uniforms, headed for the Valley River bridge. It looks like four of our little Brownies bridged to Girl Scouts this weekend! Let's hear it for the Girls!*
>
> *What's that quacking sound The Nose heard this weekend? It looks like our own mayor was a bit frustrated with the seventh hole of the local golf course and gave voice to*

his displeasure. Now now, Mr. Mayor, even in Sin-Pato we aren't Without-Manners!

Well, that was pointed, wasn't it? I looked back at the letters to the editor. The mayor wasn't much loved, at least by *Quack* readers.

Looks like all the ducklings eventually come back to the pond to roost—or is the Nose mixing her metaphors? The Nose has a big, big, big scoop for readers next week! Even a gossip columnist needs to check her sources, but she can smell a scoop at a hundred yards! And maybe a ten-year-old Simpato mystery may finally be solved.

Then my heart nearly stopped.

But for now, another duckling has flown home. Word on the street is that the Keeper's house will soon be occupied. Lady lawyer from the big city, daughter of our beloved Keeper from years gone by, may be returning to the pond soon. Readers of this column and long-time residents of Simpato will remember that the Keeper and her Drake were lost at sea, nearly ten years ago, on their sailing trip to Hawai'i. Only parts of the boat ever showed up. Will our new resident try to fill her mother's shoes, so long empty, as the new Keeper? Or will she be bringing her law practice to our little duck pond?

No wonder Carinna knew who I was. And the checker at the Duck Shop. And maybe even pickup-truck-guy. Thank goodness this Georgiana person didn't say "disgraced lady lawyer" or worse, "newly divorced and disgraced." So much for the anonymity I'd hoped for in this return to Simpato.

My soup, such as it was, was cold. I poured another glass of wine as I wondered how much that gossip columnist actually knew. Some of it was obvious, some of it accessible as a public record. Some of it, no one could ever know.

My original name was Salvia Grossman, and I later became Sal DeVine. *Sal and Saul.* Yes, very cute. Being married to Saul hadn't been all bad. There were good times, I admit. We lived quite well, perhaps better than we should have.

After the first few wild years, our marriage had been, not rocky, just dull. Convenient. We both practiced as DeVine and DeVine, each in our own separate realms: he did real estate deals, I wrote wills. Then Saul's sidelines got me into the swamp with him.

It got worse. When I learned that Saul had signed my name to both a client's property deed and the back of said client's check, with—and here was the kicker—his young and lovely intern acting as notary and bedwarmer, I told him I was filing for divorce.

The State Bar didn't give a damn about my innocence. My name was all over the documents. I was given a light sentence: two months of voluntary suspension. Saul got two years of voluntary suspension and one hundred hours of community service. Saul's relatively mild consequences only were possible if I kept quiet. If they found out about the intern it would be voluntary resignation or disbarment.

A healthy settlement from the stipulated divorce made the sixty-day suspension look cheap at the price. Until I'd had to notify my clients. And as a condition of the marital settlement agreement, I could not tell the clients who was really responsible.

Almost as if my internal narrative had summoned him, when my cell phone beeped, I knew from the personalized tone that it was Saul. Ever since the divorce he'd called me more than he had in our twenty years of marriage. *Where is this? Did I have that record? Could I get him a copy of something?* Why he couldn't just send an email was beyond me. Maybe he missed me, and the bloom was off the intern's rose. But I kept a civil tongue in my head, as my grandmother used to say. After all, my payoff for divorcing him without a fuss was that fat deposit into my separate bank account.

And to think, I would have gladly divorced him for free.

I let the call go to voicemail.

CHAPTER TWO

A restless night gave way to a beautifully clear April morning. As I was pulling on my jeans after a shower, I heard a soft knock on the door. I looked through the eyehole I had installed for my parents nearly twenty years earlier, to their hilarity. "Nothing ever happens in Sin-Pato," my dad had laughed. "That's why my law practice is so moribund."

Like me, my dad had been a lawyer and, thanks to his foresight, the house had been in their names and mine, just as their bank account had been in their names and my sister's. They must have figured my sister would need the money more than I did. Dahlia had taken after our mother and become a tarot reader on Maui. Not that Mom was a tarot reader, but she tended in that direction.

Since my parents' bodies were never found, in order to take ownership of the house under other circumstances I would have to have them declared legally dead. This way I had the house, my sister had the money, and they were, legally, alive. Just not, you know, *actually*.

I couldn't see anyone on the doorstep, so either it was a delivery and there would be an Amazon box somewhere on the step, or it was a ding-and-ditch. I'd get the delivery after I dried my hair.

Another knock, this time harder. I still couldn't see anyone through the peephole, but once I stood on my tiptoes and looked down, I caught sight of a green-covered head. Someone was out there, someone smaller even than I was. I cracked the door open.

Standing on the step was what looked like a green tent. A smallish one, narrow, about as high as my chin. "Miss Grossman?" came a voice from under the tent.

I stepped back.

"Hello?" I said, trying to peer below the surface a bit.

The tent tipped back, and a face appeared beneath a nun's wimple. Round and very white, with big, googly blue eyes shielded by thick glasses, the face broke into a smile. "Welcome back!"

"Um . . ."

"I'm Sister Sorghum, your almost-neighbor. You're Alta Grossman's daughter, aren't you?" Her voice was low and gravelly, and I bent my head to hear her.

"Sister Sorghum?" *Was that real?*

"Yes, dear. Of the Holy Order of the Little Sisters of the Earth. We were very fond of your mother. May I come in?"

What do you say to a nun who wants to come in? I stepped back, wet hair and all, and she trundled in. I could now see that it wasn't a walking tent, but a nun's habit of the old-fashioned kind, but in eco-green. From the folds she drew out a smallish cardboard box.

"Cookies," she said, thrusting it at me. "A sort of housewarming present. We sell them; that's how we maintain ourselves."

With cookies? They must have a heck of an endowment. I thanked her and put the box on the little table. "Um, would you like some coffee?" I asked.

"Oh, you just go dry your hair, dear. I'll make myself some tea and get comfortable."

"Um . . ."

"It's quite all right. I know where everything is."

"But even I don't know where I've put everything!" I said. I'd only put things away yesterday; how could she know where things were?

Sister Sorghum raised what she had of eyebrows. "But there are only a few places anyone would put tea. Think about it, dear. No matter whose house you walk into, there are no more than two, maybe three, places in a kitchen where someone would put tea."

I yielded the point, quickly vanishing into the bathroom to brush out my hair and put it into a ponytail.

"Little Sisters of the Earth?" I asked, as I reentered the kitchen. Sure enough, Sorghum here had found the mugs, the teabags I bought yesterday, and some of Saul's sweetener that had somehow hitched a ride to my house in the move. She had two cups heating in the microwave.

"Yes. We are devoted to the task of slowing climate change. Do you really use this terrible stuff?" she held up the little packet of chemicals.

I just shook my head. I couldn't go into the whole Saul business.

"So what can I do for you, Sister?" I asked, as she settled herself into the one cushioned chair in the living room. I perched on the other seat, a folding chair that was far more accommodating than it looked.

"What's your first name, dear? I can't go calling you Miss Grossman, now can I? I dearly loved Alta, you know. She was such a good Keeper. Your father was a fine gentleman, too. Especially for a lawyer. No offense meant."

"None taken," I said automatically, taking offense.

"Your name, dear?"

"Sal."

"Sal? Short for what?"

I hated this part. "Salvia."

Sister Sorghum grinned. "Ah. I should have guessed. Alta was a true friend of the earth. And do you use Grossman, or do you have a married name?" She suddenly looked around nervously. "Is there a man here?"

"None that I know of. I left him in my old place in San Francisco."

"Ah. So I thought. But did you take his name with you, along with the sweetener?"

So the nun had a sense of humor.

"DeVine."

"Oh, I couldn't possibly guess. Names are not like keeping tea in the kitchen."

"Salvia DeVine."

She spilled her tea. I jumped up to get a little square of the mopping cloths I used instead of paper towels. She was laughing, nearly rolling around in the chair. I took her tea mug, placing it carefully on the floor away from her. Side tables or a coffee table were the next order of business.

"Salvia Divinorum! Perfect! That's just like Alta, you know. Though she couldn't have guessed your married future name when you were born, could she? Unless—was it an arranged marriage, dear?" I shook my head, a little dazed. "Well, no, it wouldn't be, nowadays, young people . . . You will have to come to visit us at the monastery. You will absolutely love our mission!"

Mission? Monastery? Wasn't that for monks? Before I could frame the question politely, she had composed herself and stood. "Well, dear, *Sal,* I must be going. You must visit. Please do. Come tomorrow at noon. And we shall discuss your role as Keeper."

"Wait." I saw my chance. "What is this Keeper business, anyway? That's all I've heard since I arrived."

"Come tomorrow. We'll talk. Oh," she added as she walked out the door onto the step, "start slowly, give it at least an hour before you take a second bite."

"Bite?" I said as she made her way down the long walk.

"The cookie," she said over her shoulder. "See you tomorrow."

★ ★ ★

Names have always plagued me. Much like Sister Sorghum said, her own name being a case in itself, names are not like tea in a kitchen. You can't always imagine what the namer was thinking when they chose the name, whether self-named or bestowed by parents or fate.

Salvia Divinorum, the hallucinatory version of Salvia, or Sage, was used by natives in parts of Mexico for pain relief, digestion aids, and, of course, tripping. Regular sage, though, tends mostly to appear in Thanksgiving stuffing. Salvia is just Sage, not any specific kind.

I went by *Sal* more or less since kindergarten, as soon as kids learned the other word for *spit*, namely *saliva*. More teachers have mispronounced my name on the first day of school than I care to remember.

"Saliva Grossman" has a particularly unpleasant ring to it.

My sister, Dahlia, had gotten the better deal, though in elementary school we were quickly known as Dal and Sal.

Then there was *Sal and Saul.* Whenever anyone commented on it, I always said, "Wow! No one has ever said that before!" and waited the two beats for the person to look abashed.

Once we married, I could have stayed with Grossman, but I thought life would be easier as DeVine. Until I realized that I was now a hallucinogen.

I pondered all of that as I rinsed the teacups, eyeing the cookies on the table. She'd delivered two small cookies about the size of Oreos, one looking like chocolate chip and the other like oatmeal raisin. Thank goodness she'd warned me.

At least now I knew how the monastery supported itself. Cookies indeed.

★ ★ ★

The rest of the morning, well into the afternoon, I spent getting internet in and wifi set up, no landline needed since my cell phone would do just fine; it wasn't like I was setting up an office. At least in the short term I wouldn't need to work, since the house was mine and I did have my hush money. Though the court called it a marital settlement, rather than a payoff, Saul and I knew exactly what it was. But even prudently invested—Saul *was* a genius at that—and with a decent return, I wasn't set for life.

Besides, as someone who'd been active at something, whether it was going to school, waitressing over the summers, studying for the Bar, working as an intern or law clerk at law firms—a tale for another day, leading to marrying Saul; he *does* love his interns—to hobbies and interests, I'd never been idle.

I'd have to find something to occupy my time, whether for my sixty days of penance or permanently.

By four in the afternoon I was beat. I poured myself a glass of wine (local) and sat down on the back deck. Mount Santabella loomed to the north, lower hills flanked me both east and west, and on this Spring afternoon the sun was already hedging its bets and sneaking down toward the western range. In another hour or so Santabella would start to glow orange, its pits of old mines darkening like the carved-out eyes of a jack-o'-lantern.

The wine, though, was particularly good.

Drinking alone, on the other hand, wasn't. I put my glass down, closed my eyes.

A blast from a horn startled me awake. This afternoon

dozing had better not turn into a habit. Too many unknowns here. I looked over, recognizing the sound, and raised my hand in acknowledgment to the black pickup that had honked the daylights out of me yesterday. Another thing to put at the top of the list: I would need to put a trellis or something around the back deck. Trying to relax on the deck left me sitting there exposed to the street, yes, like a sitting duck.

"Crap," I muttered, as the black truck turned into my driveway. It was a long driveway, by town standards, because my property took up about a half-acre. The house sat roughly in the middle of the first third, leaving most of the land behind the house. The deck itself extended nicely, since my father had added terraces off it in three directions, with two steps descending to the end of the driveway.

Up those two steps the man now came, without an ounce of shyness.

"Hello there, lovely lady," he said. I reached for my phone. He saw and looked a little concerned. "Didn't mean to startle you. Just coming by to welcome you again. August," he added, holding out a hand.

"August?"

"Yep, like the month. You're the Keeper's daughter, aren't you?"

I nodded. Might as well own it, since that's what everyone was saying.

"Here to stay, or just for the summer?" he asked, looking around at the deck, with my parents' two disintegrating old mesh chaises, my good Brown and Jordan lawn furniture that I'd gotten in the divorce, and my glass of wine. He lowered himself into the other Brown & Jordan. "Your folks were great people," he said, stretching out his legs.

"Looks like you're quite comfortable," I said. "Meaning to stay for the whole season?"

August looked at me, expressionless, before closing his eyes. "Ah. Yes."

Not the answer I was looking for.

"It's been a long time, since your parents left. My Ma missed your mom something awful. I think the whole town did."

I frowned. I never knew this aspect of my mother. And now that was all I heard about.

As a kid, I never really saw my parents as real humans. They were Mom and Dad. Dahlia was close to Mom; they both liked the esoteric, but Mom had been a fourth-grade teacher most of my life, not a tarot-card reader. She did a ton of volunteer work in Sacramento, mostly teaching reading in libraries and at the prison up in Folsom, when she wasn't working or being Mom. Dad was a lawyer, wills and estates and, while I followed suit, they weren't really *people.*

When I was in law school they bought this place, and Mom spent all summer here. Dad worked in Sac, came out on weekends. I visited, but not often. They preferred coming to see me in San Francisco, staying in boutique hotels for a week and going out to dinner with me and Saul. If I visited them, it was mostly in Sacramento. The times I came here, Saul and I stayed in a nearby resort, the house not quite big enough to put us up. We have some mighty expensive resorts here in the Valley, and Saul and I enjoyed many of them.

That my mother had some sort of secret life here in Simpato was becoming obvious.

"Hey! You with us?" August spoke sharply.

"Yeah. It's just been a couple of long days, moving in and all. Thanks for stopping by, August."

He got the message. Groaning a bit, he hoisted himself to his feet. "My pleasure. Welcome to the neighborhood. I live right down the street. You'll see a lot of me!" He winked. Jeez.

"Yeah bye," I said, turning away.

"Hey! You know, I didn't get your name."

Because I didn't give it to you. "Sal," I said.

"Ok, Sally. See you tomorrow!"

"Not Sally," I started to say, then didn't bother. He was in his truck, backing up. When he got to the street, he laid on the horn one last time, and I spilled the last of my wine.

★ ★ ★

Now that I had internet, I searched the web for stories about my parents. Weird to be researching one's own family. My last name before I became DeVine was fairly common: Grossman was a rather standard Ashkenazi Jewish name, sort of a German-Yiddish *Big Guy*. Okay, it could also be *Fat Guy*, but still pretty standard issue.

More than anything, I dreaded finding any mention of me or the legal dust-up that resulted in my being here. I'd dumped Grossman pretty thoroughly when I got married, not hyphenating or turning it into a middle name, so I hoped it had vanished. Nothing jumped out regarding the legal debacle, though a quick Google of Salvia DeVine brought my law practice front and center.

I checked Saul DeVine and, though he had also managed to take a suspension, his more active role did show up in some convoluted story about the property in a legal journal. But they knew that writing trash about lawyers could have an ugly end and were careful, so the article mostly talked about the property sale and the complexities that came from it. And some cautionary moralizing at the end, because who could resist?

If I checked the Bar website it said it all in black and white: Not Eligible to Practice Law. Suspended.

I clicked out of that pretty quickly.

Anyone could find out that I was suspended. My clients all knew. Anyone with access to a computer could find out that

Saul was involved in some complicated and shady deal regarding a piece of property. But they wouldn't know about the intern. They wouldn't know about the forgery. And they definitely wouldn't know about the payoff.

Given how word spread in this little town, a place where I'd thought I could hide away until the two months had passed and I had retaken the Professional Responsibility test—another requirement, but one that I didn't worry about much, having passed it twenty years earlier with a nearly perfect score—why was I even here? Anyone who wanted to know about me would know in about three minutes.

I went back to searching my parents' names.

A couple of items popped right up: Lost at Sea; Search Called Off; Presumed Drowned. All this just a bit less than ten years ago. I remember the call. It was the strangest thing, the US Coast Guard, but with a Hawai'i area code. A soft-spoken woman gave me the news, such as it was.

I had been heartbroken, naturally, as well as surprised. My parents were amazing sailors. My dad had grown up in Massachusetts and spent his summers sailing off Cape Cod. He was used to rough waters. My mother, more traditionally raised in a New York suburb, had learned to sail with Dad and had soloed down the inland waterways of Alaska one summer.

But what I hadn't known until the call was that they'd decided to sail to Hawai'i from California. In March. Mom had retired from teaching and only had her volunteer work. She was no longer tied to a school schedule; they could have gone any time. Dad still had his practice, but he was his own boss. Estates and Trusts practices do allow for a somewhat flexible schedule, with very few emergencies that couldn't keep for a week. Plus, that kind of adventure was a crazy and involved idea that would require an enormous amount of planning.

They had a thirty-six-foot boat, a seaworthy vessel, and the experience to sail it. What they didn't do was tell me. It wasn't something that two extremely fit sixty-year-olds couldn't do; it was just something that they *wouldn't* do without telling their daughters.

Evidently they'd registered their trip with the Coast Guard. That was like them. And hadn't told Dahlia or me. That wasn't.

And yet, they'd done it. But never arrived. Never returned.

I wiped my eyes. A decade had passed, but the surprise lingered, even if I'd invented a storyline that allowed the possibility that this had been meant as a surprise. Maybe to help Dahlia bring her third kid into the world, as Dahlia didn't particularly favor husbands or marriage. But still . . .

I added "Simpato" to the search. The first result was the mythological story behind the name of the town—the white founding father had been too drunk to spell out *Simpatico*, truncating it as Simpato on the Declaration of Founding—the true story being closer to his being drunk and destroying the tribal name of the original inhabitants. The coupling of my parents' names and Simpato brought little more than the reference to their deaths.

On a whim I added Keeper.

The little dial spun a bit, and then it all popped up.

From the *Quack*, fifteen years ago: "Our Keeper Returns! This Saturday, our Keeper of Secrets opens her doors, her ears, and her lounge chair, to Simpato residents' secrets. As we've come to expect, on the third Saturday in June, Alta Grossman will be sitting on her back deck, a glass of iced tea in hand, a basket of cookies at the ready. Tissues, of course, are available. Come with your heart full, leave with a light step."

From a September issue, eleven years ago: "The last Saturday to see the Keeper, the Saturday of Labor Day weekend, is fast approaching. There's always a crush that day, with folks waiting to speak one last time, unloading their secrets to our wonderful Keeper, before she pulls in her lawn chair and returns to Sacramento. See you next June, Keeper!"

Of course, they hadn't.

From a bit over a year ago: "Georgiana Knows! What does Georgiana know about the long-ago mysterious disappearance of the Keeper? Since the Nose doesn't get involved in police matters, she's not saying, but a little quacking tells her that our mayor may have been mighty glad to see her gone. Now if he could only keep his own bill clean, Sin-Pato would be a better pond! Quack quack, Mr. Mayor!"

What the hell? Police matters?

Beyond that, there was only one more, from the BackQuack, again commemorating the loss and relating another death, this one of a local developer, in the same year.

And of course, the one from this week's the *Quack*, more or less announcing my arrival.

Tomorrow was Saturday. I was going to visit the monastery of the Little Sisters of the Earth. Maybe Sister Sorghum could enlighten me.

CHAPTER THREE

Saturday brought a late-season rain. I awoke to the *pocking* sound of water on cardboard, and the petrichor of rain on dry earth. The aroma was lovely. The realization that my boxes were getting wet wasn't.

I pulled some sweats on and ran out the back. The boxes had been pushed under the awning and were nice and dry. A moment's thought of gratitude was replaced by fury. Who had trespassed on my lot? Pushed the boxes back? My money was on August, and so was my anger. I was going have to spring for a fence, a gate, and maybe a weapon. All very unSimpato of me.

And then I thought, *wait*. The bedroom was up front; the kitchen led to the back deck. How could I have been hearing water dripping if the boxes were in the rear? I walked carefully back through the kitchen to the living room, stepping gingerly to avoid slipping on the tile with my now-wet feet, and opened the front door. There was no awning on the front, the door opened to a pair of concrete steps down to the walk, and there sat a box—cardboard guilty as charged—soaking in the drip from the gutters.

Amazon was sure quick. I picked it up. But it didn't bear the swooping smile-line of the company packaging, and the box wasn't even sealed. Someone had tucked the four panels of the top in to keep the box shut and scrawled *Sal* on the lid. I shook it but it didn't rattle or tick.

I looked around. While it was likely that August had come by the back and shoved my big, forlorn boxes under the back awning, he wouldn't likely have then come around the front to leave something for me. If anything, he would have left it in back, with the boxes.

Maybe it was more cookies. The cannabis-laced ones, or what I assumed were cannabis-laced cookies, lay untouched on my kitchen counter. I may be named for a hallucinogenic weed, but that wasn't my drug of choice.

I opened the box a little hesitantly, lest something unpleasant be lurking within. To my relief, it appeared to be a set of two tall iced-tea glasses and two long silver spoons, all carefully wrapped in thickly folded copies of the *Quack*. I checked but didn't find a note before I unwrapped the glasses. They were lovely, with stemmed California poppies etched into them, the petals painted in the signature traffic-cone orange of the flower. The leaves were a delicate green, with veins of what had to be gold paint, and the stems were a lighter green, nearly yellow.

The glasses themselves were thin, possibly crystal, though who would etch and paint fine glassware? I looked at the spoons, grabbed my reading glasses, and used my phone to magnify the inscriptions on the back of the handles. *Sterling silver, 1889.* Wow. What a gift, from whoever my benefactor was.

I put the present gently on the counter. I gathered the papers, about to toss them in my burgeoning recycling pile when the date on the paper caught my eye. It was from two weeks ago, and the headline was *Mayor Investigates Councilmember's Past.* I put that aside and leafed through the rest. What other little tidbits were hiding in the papers?

Plenty. It seemed that the mayor was in a bit of a feud with the paper's own Georgiana Noyes, also known as the

Nose. Georgiana not only wrote the local gossip column but also served on the City Council. Busy girl. The mayor, named Sebastian Solis, was being scrutinized by the Council for some alleged financial misconduct involving the bingo proceeds from the annual firefighters' fundraiser. Mayor Solis, in turn, was now conducting his own investigation of Ms. Noyes, alleging she'd been thrown off some volunteer board in a town in another county for *improprieties*. It surprised me that the story would be so vague, especially about one of its own. Leaving the peccadillo to the imagination was more inflammatory than anything she was likely to have done. It also surprised me that all this was going on in the peaceful town of Simpato.

I wondered if these papers were chosen for their topics, or whether it was just the more likely probability that they were last week's fish wrap. But they contained nothing to indicate who had given me the glasses.

★ ★ ★

A glance at my watch made me realize the morning was slipping away. I needed coffee, I needed a shower, and I needed to drop by the Sisters' monastery. Or nunnery, or convent, or whatever the word should be. I started with the coffee.

Once clean and caffeinated I slipped a rain jacket over my t-shirt, brushed the cat hair from my backside, and set out for the monastery. Sister Sorghum—I was getting used to thinking of her name without giggling—had said the place was only three blocks up from me.

The rain had stopped, and the clouds were letting a bit of blue out. The sidewalk was wet and gave off little diamonds of light where it was flat. A lot of it was uneven, where roots of what looked like maples but were actually liquid amber trees were bent on destroying the old pavement. It was treacherous walking, but the trees were budding, a gentle greening everywhere. I glanced back at my little blue cottage, seemingly afloat in a sea of delicate weeds and impending flowers. I had an unheard-of half-acre of downtown land. Anyone with that much land subdivided. Or at least grew some grapes.

Maybe I would restart my life as a viticulturist. I shook my head. I may be named for a plant, but that didn't make me a farmer.

The next two blocks were a mix of Victorians, apartment buildings, and, of all things, the back entrance to the town pool. Clearly no urban planning went into the layout of the place. All the signs in front of the pool entrance were in Spanish. I knew that the town was demographically more than fifty percent Latino, and that the entire town was divided into a third working in the wine-growing industry, a third employed in the hospitality business, and a third consisting of kids and retirees. Only about three percent were in other work, such as doctors (three), lawyers (four, or maybe now four-and-a-half), and some incredibly wealthy folks with properties valued in the tens of millions.

They were the town's benefactors, and thanks to them and according to the town website, the town boasted two public pools, a huge library, a ballroom/*quinceañera*/bingo venue, a lush park, a museum, six playgrounds, and three blue-ribbon schools. Once a year they held a dinner for all the wine folks right in the middle of Main Street, and the grandees made a speech about how wonderful Simpato was. No one ever saw them the rest of the year. They didn't get their groceries at the Duck Shop.

I arrived at the monastery, clearly something other than an ordinary house, but I didn't see any indication of religiosity or symbols of, well, whatever they believed in. An enormous dark green edifice, taking up nearly the whole block, rose from no more than three feet back from the edge of the sidewalk, giving the sense of looming grandeur, as well as flouting setback rules. I took a step backward toward the street to get an idea of what I was looking at, but I couldn't get the full view unless I crossed to the other side.

A set of heavy wood double-doors stood open at the front, and as I crossed the threshold I noticed a symbol inlaid in the marble floor. A large green tree, a conifer of some sort, stood at the center, entwined with climbing roses complete with thorns and surrounded by a clockface of fruits, most prominently grapes at twelve o'clock and green olives at six. The foyer rose what had to be three stories, and as I tipped my head back to see the top I stumbled against something soft.

"Be careful, dear," said a voice down around my middle. I regained my footing and looked down at what or who I'd stumbled against. Another green tent, another tiny nun, this one with black-framed glasses and darker skin than Sorghum's flour-white.

"Sorry, Sister," I said.

"Mother, actually. I'm the Mother Superior of the monastery, Mother Sassafras."

"As in root beer?"

She smiled thinly. "It's been said." Sort of like *Sal and Saul,* I imagined. "Welcome. You must be Alta's girl."

A forty-five-year-old girl, but yes, I nodded. It was all relative.

"Sal DeVine," I said. I didn't hold out my hand, wondering if it was proper to shake hands with a nun.

"Salvia. Yes, Sister told me about you. Come in, let me show you around. We have time before the service starts."

I hadn't signed up for a service, but I nodded again. In any event, it was too late, as Mother Sassafras was trundling off at lightning speed, turning once to urge me on.

Beyond the foyer the building opened into an outdoor

courtyard, with balconies fronting rooms on three sides. The fourth side, though, had a catwalk across it, ornately covered in wrought iron, and then reopened to the foyer, or more correctly, above the foyer.

"Up there where you were looking before," Sassafras said, "you can see our bells. They used to ring all the offices—" I frowned. "The offices of the church, dear. Matins, Compline, Vespers, you know." I tried to look knowledgeable, but although I had a greater understanding of Catholic customs than most nice Jewish girls, my own mother having been more of a pantheist than anything else, I didn't know all the terms.

Mother Sassafras was continuing. "Now we only ring them at noon, every day, and four times a day on Sunday. The City had something about ringing at four a.m. Why, I couldn't tell you. Fire engines and cop cars speed up and down this road with their sirens on at all hours, and you know that there just isn't that much crime or fire in a town of eight thousand. I think the boys just do it for fun . . ."

She was getting way ahead of me, and I sped up to catch her.

"Over here are the kitchens and the baths," she said, gesturing vaguely to the left. "The public spaces all front the courtyard. Above the baths are our dormitories. Step lively, dear, we only have a few minutes." She herself was stepping quite lively, toward the west side of the courtyard. "The conference rooms," she gestured. "Computer and media room, laboratory, lights and makeup—"

"Hunh?"

"Yes, dear. For when we give press conferences. And here's the sanctuary."

She trundled through another set of double doors, and women's voices hushed as she made her way toward the front of the room.

"Welcome to our community," Mother Sassafras said. She

showed me to a seat at the end of a carved wooden pew near the front of the room, and she herself continued to the dais up front.

In front of me were two rows of green heads, some taller than others, but all in their identical thick veils and wimples. "Welcome," they all intoned as one, in voices not much louder than a whisper, giving the word an eerie drone. I counted six to a pew, two aisles, so twenty-four nuns and a mother superior. I spotted Sister Sorghum in the front row, the smallest of them all.

Behind me were two more rows with a scattering of occupants, ranging from two teen-aged girls with impeccable long hair, one in a tube top and one in a pink tank top, to three grannies clustered together in the last row, all in what used to be called track suits in pastel colors.

The floor was marble, as the foyer was, and showed the tracks of wet and slightly muddy footsteps through the aisle. The walls soared again all three stories to the arching top, and as I sat there the bells began to ring. Noon, and time for the service.

The sense of bells echoing in my ears and head, the sound bouncing off the marble floor, and the vibration of the balconies brought to mind the Dorothy Sayers mystery where Peter finds the murderer and is almost killed by the reverberations of the bells. What was it? Right, *The Nine Tailors*. I put my hands over my ears, earning a glare from Mother.

At last the final reverberations stopped and silence, filled with auditory memory of the bells, returned. A rustle in the back made me turn in time to see two men enter and immediately go through a small door I hadn't noticed, only to appear again on the balcony above the pews. The entire room, I realized, was only women. Sort of the opposite of Orthodox Jewish services, where women were consigned to a balcony or side room, with a screen or curtain to preserve their modesty.

"Mayor," the Mother acknowledged with a small nod to the balcony. A man about fifty, with a drooping gray-and-white mustache and glasses, nodded back. He was dressed casually, in a blue plaid shirt and well-cut jeans. I couldn't see his shoes. The man next to him was taller, with broad shoulders that tapered to a narrow waist. He looked to be much younger, perhaps thirties, with blondish hair slicked down and back. If he was as old as I was, he was extremely well preserved.

The mayor whispered something to him, and the other man nodded. He followed the mayor's sightline, looked down at me, met my eyes, and winked. I felt myself redden and looked away.

Back on the dais, Mother Sassafras was gathering fronds of greenery offered to her by the nuns in the front row. A low susurration rose from the nuns and grew louder and higher in pitch as more green fronds accumulated in front of the speaker's podium, until the room was humming like a thousand bees.

Then from the left pews, the sound changed to a harmonic of the sound from the right, until that double sound merged into one textured wave of humming, gaining force as the entire room seemed to vibrate with the pitch.

And then stopped.

I exhaled.

"Preserve the earth!" Mother Sassafras said. Her words were repeated back to her from the room full of women. No baritone or bass note intruded. Even the rows of nonmonastic participants repeated her words. "Heal the earth!" "Sustain the earth!" "Heal, heal, heal!"

The crescendo of *heal* was repeated several times, until Mother Sassafras raised her little arms, then dropped them.

"Thank you. We remain committed to our cause. To reverse the despoliation of the earth." Echoes of the Passover Seder in that one, I thought.

"And now, Sister Calendula will give her report."

From the second row, a taller nun rose and made her way to the dais. When she reached the front Mother Sassafras stepped aside and took a folding chair near the first pew.

"Sisters, and Mr. Mayor," she added, as heads turned to look up at the men on the balcony, "we continue to fight the proposed development of the vineyard property at the southern base of Mount Santabella and, to that end, our mayor has agreed to interface with the city council on our behalf. As you know, the development is gaining momentum, thanks to the affordable housing mandate from the State, but we know that nothing affordable can be built so far out of town, away from the basic services and bus lines, and that only lip service will be paid to affordability."

A hand went up from one of the nuns. "Sister Marigold, in a minute, okay?" Mother Sassafras said. The hand went down.

"For an update on the council's actions, I have invited the mayor to address us today, and he will do so after our service is concluded."

"Men aren't allowed to speak during the service," said a voice behind me. I turned and saw Carinna, the White Lady, sitting behind me. She was dressed in white, of course, but instead of jeans and a long-sleeved t-shirt as she wore on Thursday, she was in a long, shapeless dress, almost a muumuu, with a deep scoop neck displaying somewhat wrinkled but ample cleavage. I nodded. Seemed right.

"Cragstown's mayor and their council are also eagerly in favor of the development, and they are ardently lobbying for moving the development closer to them, for reasons we can't discern," the hand shot up again, "although doubtless it's financial." The hand went down. "Of course, housing is already a lot more affordable in Cragstown than here in Simpato, and down the Valley, so they have less to lose."

"Typical NIMBY," whispered Carinna. "Fine for them, but not near us."

It's the other way around, I thought.

"The earth belongs to us all!" The nun who kept raising her hand finally had enough of waiting her turn.

"Sister Marigold! Please! Some decorum!" Mother Sassafras rose.

Sister Marigold strode up to Sister Calendula. "You're being too narrow-visioned! You really don't get it, do you?" Sister Marigold was as tall as Calendula, and despite the green garb she was obviously a pretty woman and could not be more than thirty. What would possess a good-looking young woman to take the veil? And this veil?

"It's about the money, honey," Marigold was saying. "The developers get rich, their council gets paid off, their mayor gets a skim, and we watch our beautiful earth destroyed. It doesn't matter if it's closer to Cragstown, or closer to Simpato. We need to take matters into our own hands and stop the big corporate interests from lining their pockets at the expense of the earth. And the small, homegrown ones too. This isn't high tea." A few giggles. "So the question is, where do we start?" Marigold turned and stomped back to her seat.

Mother Sassafras rose. "I believe we have spoken enough. We will be hearing from our own mayor and can decide on our course of action, in just a few minutes." Calendula shot a dagger look at Marigold as she made her way back to her seat.

"And now, it's my pleasure to introduce our honored guest of the day. So please welcome, with a round of applause, Salvia DeVine."

Startled, I looked up at the dais where Sassafras was beaconing me. The nuns and the non-nuns, laity I guess, were clapping and humming, and Carinna leaned forward. "Get on up there. They won't stop until you do."

Mortified, I stood and edged my way to the front. I hadn't expected to be singled out this way, nor had I planned to be in front of anyone. I had just *dropped by* as suggested.

"Welcome, Salvia. We are delighted to have you among us. Sisters, you all, or most of you," she amended, glancing down at Marigold and the nun next to her, another relatively young woman, "most of you remember our Keeper of Secrets, the dearly departed Alma Grossman." Heads bowed in memory. I glanced up at the mayor, who looked appropriately solemn. The man with him looked disengaged and was looking at his phone.

"Salvia is her daughter. She's returned to Simpato just this week. We are delighted to have a Keeper once again. Will you be hearing us on Saturdays and Sundays, as your mother did, or will you be having evening and weekday hours as well?"

"Um . . ." I said.

Sister Marigold stood up. Sassafras frowned. "How do we know she can be trusted?" Marigold asked. "Who the hell is she, anyway?"

A gasp rose from the room, and in the back, the two teen-aged girls giggled and hugged themselves.

"She's the Keeper's daughter," Sister Sorghum said, from the front. "That means she's fit for the job. And we need a Keeper."

"Um . . ." I said.

"She's a lawyer, so how does that make her trustworthy?" the little young nun next to Marigold said. "In fact that makes her less than trustworthy, in my opinion."

"Enough!" Mother Sassafras said. "Unless you want to do penance for the rest of the weekend, you'll keep a civil tongue in your mouth." Second time I'd heard that in two days. Must be a thing here, I thought, my mind grasping at anything but what was going on. "Salvia, I apologize for the graceless behavior of some of my Sisters. Please, the floor is yours. We eagerly await your words."

I fumbled for a moment. "Uh, thank you, Mother Sassafras." Then my inner lawyer kicked in. "I have, er, very little to add to your warm welcome. As you know, I just arrived two days ago, and have only just had the pleasure of meeting you and Sister Sorghum. As to my mother, yes, indeed, um . . . well, may her memory be a blessing." I thought I heard a snicker from the balcony, but didn't look up.

"My mother was so fastidious in her role as Keeper of Secrets that she never breathed a word of this to me, or, as far as I know, to my sister Dahlia." I need to text her, I thought. We weren't in touch much, but texting worked. "So I will need your guidance as to what's involved. But as to trustworthiness, I assure you that anything that anyone tells me stays with me. Regardless of what you might see on television, we lawyers have absolute rules about confidentiality, which I honor."

Again the snicker, and this time I did look up. The mayor was watching the back of the room, not even looking at me, but the man he was with was holding his phone, and his smile was disconcertingly smug. I could only guess what he'd found.

"Thank you, my dear. I'm sure you'll let us know what the schedule is," Mother Sassafras was saying, in a tone that meant I was done and could go sit down.

"Our concluding hymn," Mother Sassafras was saying.

I sat back down. "Nice going," Carinna whispered. "Sassafras sandbagged you, but you slipped out from under." I turned to answer her but the humming started. Again it rose in tone, and then, like bees in a hive, the sound appeared to swarm around me. It was nearly a physical experience, and intensely unnerving.

Then the nuns rose and began to leave single file, first the right-side front row, then the left, followed by the second rows. As Marigold passed me, she stopped humming and mouthed, "I'll call you," as she went by. I nodded, though I didn't know why she would want to, especially after openly challenging my integrity.

I took another glance at the balcony, despite trying very hard not to. Both men were gone. In the back of the room, as the nuns walked by, the grannies were whispering, and behind them a tall woman with unnaturally red hair was leaving as well.

"Who's that?" I whispered to Carinna. "With the red hair?"

"Georgianna Noyes. The Nose. You know. The gossip columnist."

The gossip columnist, city-council member, and the mayor's foe. Quite a number of hats for one person. "I wonder what she was doing here at the monastery."

"Politics and gossip are everywhere," Carinna said, in a regular tone of voice. "You'll be in the column again this week, guaranteed.

CHAPTER FOUR

"Want to go for a walk around No-Duck Lake?" Carinna said as we exited.

"Shouldn't we wait to hear the mayor speak?" We both looked around. "I wonder where he'll give his comments," I added. "I thought he would be addressing the group right in the—what do you call it?"

"They call it the Service Hall, but it was the chapel when this was an actual Catholic monastery. No, they can't have men speak in the Service Hall. He would have to be up on the balcony, here in the foyer, or in a conference room, depending on how many people stay for it. We can, if you want."

"Yeah," I said. "I might as well find out what this is all about. I got the sense that the nuns' concerns were more about *where* rather than *if* there would be development. It didn't seem like the typical *eco-warriors versus developers* argument."

Carinna shook her head. "It's a variation on a theme. The State wants affordable housing. They've ordered that every town add a certain percentage, even a little place like Sin-Pato. And even though half our population, more or less, already lives in old apartments where the rent hasn't been raised in five years."

"How do you know that?" I asked, softening my tone and looking as doe-eyed as I could. That kind of question always comes off as challenging, at the very least. Offensive wasn't far behind. But I really wanted to know.

"Easy. I own two of them. Buildings. The issue of development comes up every few years here. There's been plenty of talk pro and con at the past few city council meetings."

"I guess the town could always use a few more units," I said cautiously.

"Some do-gooders in town definitely want more. Generally, the eco-nuns want to stop any more development of any sort, since the only places to go from here are out or up. Up the mountain or out into the vineyards. Take out vineyards and green spaces. Before the State said we had to add housing, getting approval was a tough fight. The last time anyone had a project approved, um . . . he died. Not because of his development," she added quickly. "I mean, no one ever figured out why—" She glanced around anxiously.

"So what's the problem with this new proposal, from your point of view?" I asked, redirecting the conversation.

"The developer that put in the bid to do the most recent housing project has been pressuring the town to pay all kinds of costs for them—like land prep and engineering. They've got us sort of over a barrel because of the State. To the north, the nearest town, Cragstown, is happy to accommodate the developer, but they don't have anywhere near the kind of money that the Duck has to do that size of a project."

This was leading me to more questions: what percentage of the housing would be "affordable"? What did that even mean? And what about the rest of the development? How luxurious would that be?

"But wouldn't a big development put a lot of strain on services?" I asked. "I mean, there's only one supermarket, and that barely accommodates the town as it is. And busses?"

"All been raised at council meetings. Shut down or ignored.

The Nose wants it to go forward, and she knows how to push. Or shove. Where the hell's the mayor?" Carinna asked. She craned her neck and scanned the area. "He's not up on the balcony. Let's check the conference room."

Nuns were milling around outside the conference room, with a table with cookies and lemonade ready, but the room itself was empty.

"He hasn't shown up yet," said one nun. "Neither has Georgiana."

"Is there a men's room?" I asked. "He had already left when you all buzzed out."

I meant it to be funny, but she took it in stride. "We do have a restroom for anyone to use, but those two young ladies," she said, indicating with a glance the two giggling teenaged girls, "just came out of there, so if he was in there—well, he wouldn't have been."

Sister Sorghum came bustling up to us. "I just don't know where Mayor Solis has gotten to. He seems to have disappeared. And we were so looking forward to his discussion. He's a true eco-warrior. It would be so wonderful for you to hear him."

"There was another man with him," I said cautiously. I hadn't liked the look of that smirk, handsome though the guy was. "Maybe he left with him."

"Oh, Scooter? He's the local librarian. I doubt he went anywhere with Scooter."

Scooter? Librarian?

"A regular customer," Sorghum added. "Oh! Mother! Do you know what's happened to the mayor?"

"Happened? Has something happened to the mayor?" Mother Sassafras, so unflappable in the Service Hall, appeared to panic.

"Not what I meant, Mother. Just asking if you knew where he might be."

Mother Sassafras composed herself quickly. "No, Sister. I don't. I expected him here in the conference room, ready to address us."

We milled around for a bit longer. Some took cookies; some took lemonade. Given the *funny cookies* I wasn't going to take either.

"Let's go for our walk," Carinna said. "Nothing is happening here."

"Let me go back to my house, put on some different shoes."

"Good idea, it will be muddy after last night's rain. I'll meet you at the corner of Peaches and Second in, what? Half-hour?"

I tried to remember where Peaches was. My house backed up to Second Street, three blocks from here. "It's about six blocks north on Second," Carinna said, headed for the exit, carefully sidestepping the grapes at twelve o'clock. "See you there."

"Before you go," a hand on my shoulder stopped me. I looked up at Marigold. "Can I have a word?"

★ ★ ★

Sister Marigold drew me into a little room just past the restroom. The other, younger nun she'd been walking with slipped in behind us, gripping two tall glasses of lemonade. I eyed them warily.

"Would you like some lemonade?" the non-Marigold nun asked, holding out a glass. I shook my head.

"Sorry about the public challenge," Marigold said, sounding like a normal millennial of some sort. "It was just to throw off Calendula. She's soooo sure of herself."

"Smug, you know?" said the other one, with a strong Valley-Girl intonation. San Fernando Valley, Moon-Beam Zappa Valley. Not our Valley.

"Oh, sorry. Gingerroot."

"Seriously?" I said before I could stop myself.

"Seriously," Sister Gingerroot said. "*To*-tally smug."

Whew.

"Sure you don't want some lemonade?" Gingerroot asked again.

Marigold slid me a wink.

"We just want to know where you stand on this," Sister Marigold picked up the conversational ball. "Are you for the issue? Against it? Undecided?"

"We can help you with that if you are," Sister Gingerroot chimed in.

"Totally," Marigold added, with a sly eyebrow raise. This one bore watching.

"I don't know enough about it," I said. "I just moved in."

"And you just happen to own a half-acre of in-town property, with a teensy-weensy little house on it, that you could sell to the developer for a fortune. It would be the ideal place to put up a nice five-story apartment building, full of affordable units, and leave our mountain and our valley alone!"

Ah.

"But that was my parents' home," I started. And besides, unless I had them declared dead, I didn't have exclusive owner-ship. I couldn't sell it. Though after nine years, and an obituary, a *shiva*, a celebration of life, it wouldn't be that hard to get a court to declare them dead. They were dead. And I could get a lot of . . .

"Yeah, but you haven't lived there, like, ever," Gingerroot said, interrupting my thoughts.

Marigold laid a hand on her green-covered arm. "Let her think about it, Ginger." She smiled a tight little smile at me. I felt like she was seeing me naked, and I felt myself blush.

"We'll be in touch," she said, and again, it was those eyes. Long and brown, with thick lashes, lightly lowered at me.

I shivered. "I promise."

She guided Sister Gingerroot out the door, leaving me flummoxed and alone in the little side room.

* * *

I got out of there before anyone else could waylay me. This was the strangest convent I could ever imagine. I walked quickly back to my house, not even looking up at the now-clearing sky, concentrating on not slipping on the walkway to my house. I let myself in and saw the newspaper I'd left on the chair. I'd forgotten to ask Sister Sorghum about the beautiful etched glasses.

I looked at the article again. The mayor was being accused of skimming funds from the city. Georgiana Noyes certainly didn't have a high regard for the head of the city, neither as gossip columnist nor as councilwoman. I wondered what side of this development mess she was on. And about the mayor. "Mayor Solis is a great eco-warrior." That's what Sister Sorghum—or was it Mother Sassafras—had said.

Those names were preposterous. And Marigold? Gingerroot, for crying out loud?

And the librarian, what was it? Speeder? No. Scooter. That was no librarian I'd ever seen.

I put my sneakers on and hung my rain jacket on the hook near the door. I looked at my phone, which I'd had on *silent* during my visit to the monastery. Two texts from Saul. The first wanted to know where I'd packed his golf shoes. *We're not married anymore, dude,* I wanted to text back. Besides, I hadn't packed his stuff. The second was a picture of Luna, sitting on a green cushion, licking her paw. Was he rubbing it in?

We'd split up the majority of the stuff easily. I had picked out most of the furniture throughout our marriage, but none of it was new, none of it fancy. I was moving into 900 square feet; he was moving to a gorgeous Victorian in Alameda. I let him take everything except the Brown Jordan patio furniture. That, I said, was mine.

"Okay," he'd said. "But I get the cat."

The cat? I had been outraged. Sure, we both loved the cat, but how dare he? Luna belonged with me.

"Nope," he'd said. "I get the cat. At least until you're reinstated by the Bar. If you ever are. And I wouldn't fight me on that," he'd added.

I hadn't been able to figure out why he'd done that, until I saw the Insta account of his, or our, or make that *his*, intern. There were at least five photos of her with the cat. In our condo. I had taken the patio furniture and left. And now he was taunting me with the cat?

I shook my head. The damned cat had completely distracted me from the whole business at the monastery, never mind changing my shoes.

I'd just gotten the second sneaker tied when I heard the now-familiar horn blast. I didn't have time for August right now. I went out the back, and sure enough his black pickup truck was screeching to a halt at the end of my drive.

"I was just heading out," I called to him.

He jumped down from the truck cab. "Hey. No prob. I just wanted to share a secret or two. When you coming back?"

"Look, August. I haven't come to terms completely with this new role yet," I said.

"No prob," he said again. "I'll walk you through it. I used to come with my Ma all the time. I know how it's done."

"Thanks, August. I think I'll start next weekend, though. This is a little too soon."

August looked down. "Aw, okay. I understand," he said. "I guess I'll just wait then. You sure?"

"Positive, August. Now, I've got to get going."

He shuffled his feet. "Did you like that I moved your boxes for you? They were getting wet." I nodded. "What've you got in there, anyway? Bricks?"

"Books," I said.

"Same diff," he answered. "Can I drop you anywhere?"

"Where's Second and Peaches?"

"Not too far, about six blocks."

I looked at my watch. Carinna would be there already.

"I can take you. It's right at the entrance to the trail around No-Duck."

I wondered if I was taking my life in my hands. "Okay. Let me lock up."

He laughed. "Lock up? No one locks their doors in Sin-Pato. There's no crime here. Safe as a bank."

I thought about all the bank robberies in the world. I grabbed my keys and locked the doors.

"Careful getting in," he said, opening the truck door for me in a gentlemanly move. He put his hand under my elbow to help hoist me. He must think I'm ancient. On the other hand, it was a big step for someone five-two.

He slammed the door after me and hopped in the other side.

"To the Lake!" he said. "What an honor, to be driving the Keeper around town!" He laid on the horn. "Hey everyone!" he shouted out his window, honking the crap out of the horn. "Look who I've got! Whooohooo!"

★ ★ ★

Carinna's face was worth the mortification of the ride, as we pulled up within an inch of her feet on the sidewalk. "August Sanjusto! What the hell do you think—"

"Hey, White Lady!" August hollered out his window. "Look who I brought! I brought the Keeper!" Before I could request otherwise, August was out of the truck and around the cab to my door. "My lady," he said, bowing me out.

"Thanks for the ride," I said. "See you next weekend."

"Oh, I'm sure I'll see you before that! I mean, I live only a coupla houses down from you, you know. Me and my Ma." He turned to Carinna. "See ya, White Lady."

"Don't honk the—"

"Never on Sunday" drowned out the remainder of my request as he roared off down Second.

"Jeez Louise," Carinna said. "I don't think he'll ever grow up. This way," she added. The path left the sidewalk and led past the abandoned campground, its hookup posts now decaying in the sun, wires hanging every which way. "Any copper in the wires was stolen long ago," she said.

The paved trail emerged at the edge of a reedy waterway, greenish in the afternoon light. We took the left fork, and walked in silence for a few minutes. It was peaceful, just a block from Second Street, with the Spring growth of weeds and emerging wildflowers. I saw little pink ones, what looked like buttercups only more open, and the beginning of the California poppies, the State flower, with their orange petals against dark green fronds. Soon there would be a riot of them, but now only a few shy early bloomers popped against the more sedate background.

As we rounded the first corner, the lowest slopes of Mount Santabella rose in front of us. "I had no idea we were so close to it," I said. The first part had some terraced vineyards, before the landscape grew harsh and rocky.

"Right here at hand. No-Duck Lake is actually part of the water purification system," Carinna said, gesturing toward the water. "The water naturally collects here and is augmented by the pipes that trap the water from the vineyards running off the mountain. The water goes into the next pond, a manmade one. It's aerated—see the fountain in the middle? That's aeration. And then it's sent off to irrigate the vineyards again. Not drinkable, not potable water, though it might taste better than Simpato's faucet-juice, but definitely reusable."

"Doesn't it flow into the Valley River?"

"Not supposed to, no. They get fined if it does. Too much sediment and salt."

The water looked pure and fresh. You never knew.

"I noticed that the water from the taps tastes like dirt," I said.

"If they can afford it, over half of the Simpato population buys its water. It's the other half that has to drink it. Like everything else. Want to walk up the mountain a ways?"

I nodded and we branched off the main trail, leaving the paved way for a gravel path that led along a vineyard. The vines were just budding green, the dirt was freshly turned and damp from the morning rain, and the sun was shining. In the distance I could hear crows, and closer in a bird was yipping away. Flies and other buzzing insects were hovering around the new leaf buds. All it needed was Julie Andrews and Dick Van Dyke singing "Jolly Holiday" from *Mary Poppins* to make the scene complete.

"You doing okay?" Carinna asked. I nodded. "Want to keep going up?"

I had to admit I was out of shape for hiking, after hiding away in my condo for six months. Normally frequent walking of San Francisco's hills kept me fit, but I'd spent the whole winter ignoring the world and burying myself in work, books, and misery.

"Just a bit more, then," Carinna said.

I looked at the dry rocky area above us, with only one tall tree, the rest just shrubs. "Just to the end of the vineyards. It doesn't look all that interesting up there."

"Okay," she said. "There's a couple of little caves where the rocks have eroded, and some abandoned mine pits, and sometimes you can find what looks like gold. It's actually pyrite, fools' gold, you know, but it's pretty. And who's to say?"

"That would be fun," I said. "Don't the Girl Scouts or someone give tours up here?"

Carinna laughed. "No, not the Girl Scouts, bless their mercenary little hearts. If they can't sell it, they don't do it. Tours are through the historical society at the library. Scooter gives the tour on the third Saturday of the month. You should do it. It's fun."

That would be next Saturday. I wasn't sure I wanted to spend time with "Scooter," though, and his smug phone.

"He's a real historian," Carinna was saying. "He knows everything about the town. The joke is he knows where the ducks are buried."

At the end of the vineyard we stopped. I took a couple of breaths, looked down at the valley below me. It was a perfect light green, the blue of the lake reflecting the clearing sky. So peaceful. I looked up at the sky, closed my eyes. Which is why I didn't see Carinna keep going. It wasn't until I heard her scream that I opened them again.

I whirled around to look for her, but she was nowhere to be seen. "Carinna!" I shouted.

"Oh my god!" I heard from nearby. "Oh my god! Sal!"

"What? What is it? Where are you?"

"Up here!"

I looked up a bit, but then saw that off to my right, away from where I had been looking, her white pants were visible around a bush. Why had it seemed like her voice was coming from the left, though? I headed off the path toward her, scrambling a bit on the loose rock. I grabbed a piece of plant to steady myself, and it came off at its roots. I stumbled forward, catching my jeans on a prickly bush. I felt it scratch my arm, and I pulled away sharply.

With that motion, the ground gave way and I slid down a few feet off the path. Everything I grabbed at had prickers, and I could see blood running down my arm from the scratches. How had Carinna gotten there in a few seconds?

I scrambled around the next bush, where I could see Carinna's white clothing, and stopped. It wasn't Carinna. It was a white shirt, or blouse, caught on a branch, waving emptily in the faint breeze.

I grabbed the shirt and wrapped it around my bleeding arm. It was a woman's blouse, soft and delicate, but not small.

"Sal! What are you doing over there?"

I turned back to where I'd come from, and there was Carinna, waving madly. I made my way back to her. "Sorry, I thought you were over on this side but it was the white shirt . . ."

Carinna was pale and breathing a lot harder than I had been walking up the slope. "Sal. Jesus. Come on, we've got to get down."

"What?"

"Oh shit. Come and see." This time I followed her about ten yards, then she ducked into a little cave.

"So that's why I couldn't see you," I said.

"Look."

I looked down where she was pointing. "Oh god." It was a leg—a long leg in grey denim. Attached to the back of an obviously female torso, since it wore a bra back, but no shirt. And though I couldn't see beyond the back of the shoulders, there was long red hair. Lots of long red hair.

I felt my meager breakfast in the back of my throat. Then I looked at the blouse, with my blood on it. Breakfast exited.

"Okay, let's go get help," I said, after a quick retch. I reached into my back pocket for my phone.

"No reception up here," Carinna said. "There never is. They'll have to add it if they build condos down there." She was babbling.

"Down we go, then."

"One of us should stay here with her," she said, "so, I don't know, animals don't get her." I gagged. "I know the way down. You stay here."

I wanted to say no. I wanted to say that we could both go, but I also knew she was right. "Okay but be quick."

"I'll come back as soon as I've called. I can get reception not too far from here."

She headed back down the hill.

Wait, I thought. We hadn't even tried to see if the woman was alive, or if we could help. I edged back into the cave and carefully knelt down. I put my hand on the woman's back. No response. She was cool to the touch, but then she was lying there without a shirt on a seventy- degree day.

"Hey," I said. "Are you okay?" That sounded stupid even to me. I could see that her other leg was bent under her, in a bad position. If she was alive, she wasn't conscious, or she'd be in a whole lot of pain.

I had no experience with this sort of thing. In my law practice, by the time folks needed to see me the decedent they were inheriting from was well past this point. Should I try to turn her over? Find a pulse?

"It's going to be okay," I said to the woman. If she wasn't dead, help was on the way.

★ ★ ★

But she was dead.

Carinna returned, and moments later two policemen followed. I stepped aside and let them do their job.

"Stay over there, ma'am," one of them said. I moved to where he was pointing, out of the way and still in sight. "You can sit down on that rock. Sergio, take a look." The other policeman squeezed in next to the first one.

"Ay, holy shit, man." He emerged and took out his radio. Soon there were five or six people in various uniforms, some photographing, one talking into his shoulder, and a young man and a more mature woman turning the person over.

"Jesus Mary and Joseph," the first cop said. He crossed himself. The policeman he'd called Sergio turned away and, like I had, lost his lunch. I didn't think police did that, but they were human, and Sergio was pretty young.

When the two paramedics pulled the body out of the cave I could see why. I could also see who.

Georgiana Noyes, the gossip-columnist city-councilwoman, lay in her bra and jeans, barefoot, with her forehead bashed in.

* * *

At the police station, I sat in a room with a window that looked out to the parking lot, covered by a venetian blind with the slats open. There were four wooden chairs, a table with a paper cup of water, and a photo of the governor and an American flag on the wall. I sat in one chair, and the first policeman, whose name tag showed L. Aureliano, sat in the second chair.

We were joined by a third man, in a green shirt, khaki pants, and sneakers. No name tag, no tie. This wasn't "LA Law." It was Without a Duck, California.

"Mrs. DeVine," said the man in green, "I'm chief of police Devon Plata. He put out a hand, and well-brought-up that I was, I shook it. I might as well. I was shaking everything else too.

"Salvia DeVine," I said.

"Would you like coffee or something?"

I shook my head. But that was because I couldn't control it. "Sorry. Yes, please. I just can't stop shaking."

Chief Plata looked over at Aureliano. He shrugged, got up, and returned moments later with another paper cup, this one filled with what might have been sludge, might have been coffee once.

"The water isn't that great," Plata said. "I don't blame you."

I took a sip. It was espresso. It was delicious. It also helped. Within a minute or so I had stopped shivering.

"Better?" I was able to nod coherently at the question. "Good. Because we have to ask you for some details, and it would be a lot easier for both of us if you can sit still long enough to answer them." He smiled. He was a nice-looking man, blue-eyed, brown-haired, muscular without being muscle-bound, with a hooked nose and pleasantly full lips.

I pulled myself together. What the hell was I doing, ogling the Chief of Police, when I had just found the body of a local councilwoman? It must be the shock.

He smiled. He was probably used to it.

"Okay. Let's get started." He turned to the other man. "Ready, Luke?"

Officer Aureliano pushed a button on a digital recorder. Chief Plata identified himself, as did Officer Luke Aureliano, and asked me to give my full name and spell it. He asked me for my address. It took a moment to remember to give the Simpato address, not the San Francisco condo. He noticed the hesitation with a flick of his eyebrows but didn't remark on it.

Plata led the conversation. He also took notes on a little yellow steno pad, but mostly he looked kindly at me. "Okay, can I call you Salvia?"

"Sal is what I go by, mostly."

"Sal, then. And you can call me Devon. Never liked the nicknames it brought on." A little smile. I acknowledged it with a nod.

"Let's start with the basics, give me a little background so I can know you a bit, then I'll help you tell us exactly what you saw this afternoon. And any time you want more coffee, or need a bio-break, just say the word. We want you to be comfortable and be able to access all of what you sensed and saw. And I know it's hard, after that sight. So we'll take our time, okay?"

Once again, he checked for buy-in, and I nodded. "So, what brought you to Simpato?"

I glanced at Aureliano. Didn't everyone know who I was,

after all? He just looked at the recorder. "I'm Salvia DeVine, I'm the daughter of Alta and Stanley Grossman, who used to have the house on Main at Second Street. I just moved back to Simpato—" I stopped. Did I?

"I actually used to visit my parents occasionally when they lived here, but as you know they left on a sailing trip in March about nine years ago and were lost at sea. Since then, I only came by once a year for an afternoon to check that the house was okay, you know, the roof wasn't leaking or anything. But this week I moved my stuff in. So I'm living there now."

That felt more comfortable, less permanent.

"And your husband, Mrs. DeVine?" Luke Aureliano asked.

Devon Plata frowned a briefest of scowls.

"I'm divorced."

Plata shifted his body so he was more facing me, less sideways to Aureliano. Kind of an *I'm in charge here* signal to his subordinate. "Ok, Sal, now that you're here, what did you do this morning?" I looked at him, cocking my head to the side. A silent *why?* "Trying to get some context," he said.

"Um, I went to see the monastery."

"Ah. Our Little Sisters of the Ecology," he said.

"Of the Earth," Aureliano corrected. Plata ignored him.

"How long did you stay?"

"Until the end of their service, around one in the afternoon." I decided to short-circuit this lengthy dialogue. "I was invited by the woman called Sister Sorghum. She suggested I drop by around noon, and so I did. I had no idea about a service, as they called it, nor anything other than to see the monastery, or whatever the public parts of it are, and say hello. But apparently they expected me. I was collared by Mother Sassafras—"

"Oh yes, she can be extraordinarily persuasive," Devon Plata said. "You should see her fundraising at Community Bingo."

Community bingo?

"So I went in to their little, er, chapel, and watched the

service. I was introduced, because my mother was Alta Grossman, and she seems to be known around town as the Keeper. I never knew about this role of hers, but it's been constant since I arrived."

"That's what I thought," Devon Plata said. "The Keeper's daughter."

"Can you tell me more about that?" I asked.

"Maybe when we're done. Let's stay on task." As if I'd diverged. "So you stayed for the service then decided to go up Mount Santabella?"

"No, not exactly."

"Stay for milk and cookies?" Aureliano interrupted.

I guessed that the snacks were a regular part of the event.

"No. I thought the mayor was supposed to speak, I guess about the development that's controversial, but he had left—"

"Left? He was there?"

I nodded. "He was up in a balcony, I guess men don't sit with women there."

Aureliano nodded. "Men sit in the balcony. Who else was up there? Any other guys?"

This time Plata didn't fuss.

"A man that was later identified to me as *Scooter* the librarian." Plata groaned quietly. "In the back of the chapel, on the main floor, the lady we found on the mountain, the gossip columnist, she was there too."

Both cops were looking at me intensely. "You're sure about that?" Plata said, writing on his notepad.

"Absolutely. Or at least that's who Carinna said it was." I realized that I had no independent knowledge of the woman's identity.

"Carinna?"

"The woman I was walking with. The one they call the White Lady. Because she wears white, I guess."

Aureliano splurted a laugh. "Sort of. If you noticed, Simpato is only half white. And most of us who aren't white are Hispanic. And Karen is definitely a white lady."

I shook my head, but Plata put a hand up. "Later. Later. Now we need to cover the finding of the body. So, you and Carinna," he swallowed as he said her name, "left the monastery and went walking?"

"No. I went home, to my, to my house, changed my shoes, and met her at the entrance to the walking path around Simpato Lake. At two." Both cops made notes. "I got a lift over there from a neighbor who'd stopped by. August. I don't know his last name, but he drives a black pickup—"

"Like half the guys in this town," Aureliano said. "And he lays on the horn like he's the trumpeter in the mariachi band." I nodded. "He's a little different," Aureliano added. "But hey, we don't judge."

Like hell you don't.

Plata was tapping impatiently on his pad with his pen. "Back to this afternoon, please." His voice was crisp this time, and Aureliano sat back in his seat. The displeasure was clearly directed at him. I wasn't going to mess with this.

"August lives, apparently, a few houses down from me. He stopped by, and he's done that before, and said hello, and offered me a ride. I took it because I was supposed to meet Carinna at two and it was already two, I don't have her cell phone because I just met her, and I didn't want to keep her waiting. Once I got to the path, she and I walked around the lake to the trail going up the mountain. She asked if I wanted to keep going, I said yes, but only to the end of the vineyard. We got there, I was a little out of breath, and we stopped to rest. I turned to admire the view, and next thing I heard her scream. I joined her and we saw the woman on the ground, but I didn't realize it was the woman we saw at the services. I stayed with her, and Carinna went down to call you."

Plata nodded. "Okay, good. That's very helpful. About how long from when you started your walk until you found the victim?"

"I don't know, I guess less than an hour, because it wasn't that long a walk."

"And you went straight to the cave where she lay? Why?"

Oh, shit. "No. I didn't."

"Explain, please," Devon said, and he was not Devon, suddenly, he was all *Chief Plata* in his question.

"It's hard, kind of confusing. I had been looking at the view, and then I heard Carinna scream. I turned around, and it sounded like it came from my left. But I saw white clothing to my right. And Carinna wears white, so I thought maybe I had been mistaken. So I started to go to my right, but there wasn't really a path. I slipped, and scrambled down the hill a little, and a bush cut my arm." I held out my arm, where yes, a small scratch showed. I remembered it as much larger.

"It was bleeding, so I grabbed the white cloth, which turned out to be a white blouse, and wrapped it around my arm. Carinna was yelling for me to come to her, and I realized that what I originally thought, that Carinna had gone left on the path, was right. I mean, *correct*. I made my way back, it was only a very short distance, but she had been inside the little cave so I couldn't see her. Once I got there, I saw the victim. But I didn't know she was dead, although I guess I should have, the way her leg was bent. Carinna went to get help. I, um, puked."

Plata nodded sympathetically. "You'd be amazed at how many junior officers do too, the first few times. Especially with a recent kill."

There was a term I hadn't heard before. "One of them did," I said.

Aureliano nodded. "Sergio."

"Poor kid," Plata said. "So, you waited for Carinna to go get help. Why didn't you go with her?"

"We thought someone should stay with the, um, yeah, and she said she knew the way, so I stayed. In case of animals . . ."

"And . . ."

"And nothing."

"Did you touch her?"

"No. Wait, yes. I put my hand on her back. I realized we didn't even know if she was dead or alive. But I put my hand on her, and she felt—I don't know—dead."

Plata nodded. "What did you do with the blouse?"

I looked at him. I thought. He waited. I shook my head. "I have no idea."

He continued to look at me. I shook my head again.

He sighed. "All right. Just one last question."

I was right to think of Columbo then.

"Why didn't Carinna call 911 from there?"

Whew. An easy one. "Because there's no cell service up there."

Aureliano burst out laughing. "Sure there is, lady. They've got the whole infrastructure for the freakin' development all set in. The only tall tree nearby is a cell tower."

"That's enough," Plata said. "Why don't you go home and get some sleep. It's been a terrible day for you. Tomorrow I might have some follow-up questions, though, so don't leave town, okay?" He laughed as he said it. He wasn't kidding though, and we both knew it.

"Should I take her home?" Aureliano asked.

Plata shook his head. "No need. There's no crime in Simpato."

CHAPTER FIVE

Simpato and the Valley are known for their wine, and this evening certainly called for some anesthetic. I poured myself a glass of Malvasia, a white with significant floral notes, and drank the whole thing without a single floral acknowledgment.

Unfortunately, I'm not used to drinking much, and immediately after I finished the glass I realized that I hadn't eaten since breakfast, which I'd barfed on the mountain. I hadn't had anything to drink, either, other than that delicious espresso at the police station. I set about making some food, and chewed a piece of sourdough bread torn from the loaf, hoping it would absorb some of the wine now sloshing unpleasantly in my stomach.

I fixed a salad and took the rest of the bread and made French toast, about all I could handle tonight in both the cooking and the eating departments, then settled down at my little table to eat.

The box with the two cookies was still there. I remembered Officer Aureliano's remark about the milk and cookies. Right. I'd forgotten that the Little Sisters supported themselves with pot pastries. I assumed legally. But if I'd had one, it would certainly have made my recollections a lot less trustworthy.

I now realized that he wasn't just shooting his mouth off

during Plata's questioning of me as a witness. He was there for a purpose, and his comments had been, for the most part, expected. Though maybe he was enjoying his role a bit too much. Plata sure snapped him back when he went off on Carinna.

My mind swirled with all the new people and input it had. Which conveniently obscured the fact that I had found a dead woman today.

★ ★ ★

I woke up in the chair in my living/dining room with a stiff neck, a headache, and an idea. I checked my phone and, seeing that it was two in the morning, put my thoughts into the notes app and made my way to bed. Tomorrow, or actually today, it would be Sunday, and I hoped everything would be a little quieter.

★ ★ ★

Sunday dawned clear and calm. The unsettled weather had passed. Maybe the unsettled events had passed too. I made coffee and googled fencing companies—the kind that built fences, not the kind that dueled with epées or sold stolen goods. Out here in Simpato there was nothing, but if I widened my search it showed plenty of companies in the main city, Valley. And one in Cragstown. What an unmelodiously named city.

Maybe today I'd drive around a bit and check out the area, including that sorry-sounding place. And first thing Monday I'd see about getting a fence put in, at least along the driveway side of the house. With one of those smooth electric gates, one that slid silently back and forth with the touch of a remote control. Sort of a country garage-door opener.

That brought to mind the fact that there was no garage, no place to store things. I checked for the number for the storage facility that I'd seen right outside of downtown. They were open on Sundays until three. Excellent. I'd load the three boxes up into my car and go rent a storage unit. Then I'd head over to check out Cragstown and maybe even go see where the development everyone was all excited about in the gossip column was supposed to be going up. And then—

I remembered that Georgiana Noyes was dead. No more gossip columnist. No more column.

I was rinsing my coffee cup when the horn blasted. I was going to have to tell August not to do that anymore. And I really needed to get a gate.

Sure enough, there was the black truck right at the end of the walkway from my deck to the driveway. He was hopping out of his side, bouncing his way to my door. I beat him to it.

"Sally! I heard the news!"

"It's Sal, August. And could you not lay on the horn when you come visit?"

"Sorry, Sally. Sal. I like Sally better. I'll try to remember."

"Try to remember both things, August. That my name is Sal, and that you shouldn't blare your horn when you pull up. It, it startles me."

August looked down at his feet. I felt a little guilty. He wasn't completely "there," I knew. He looked just fine, in his jeans, Keds, and an old Simpato Ducks t-shirt, and his brown hair was neatly cut, but he wasn't quite . . . quite.

"Thanks, August. Say, could you do me a favor?"

He perked up immediately. "Sure, *Sal*."

"Can you put those three boxes in my car?"

"Of course I can," he said. "In that red car?" There wasn't any other car in the parking gravel. I nodded. "They won't all fit."

"Sure they will," I said. "You can turn them sideways or something."

He shook his head. "They won't. I know this. I'm really, really good at putting things in trucks. That's my job, you know. I load trucks." I hadn't known. "And I'm sure they won't fit."

I shrugged. "Okay, just put the ones that will fit in there." I figured I'd make two trips. Though it did look to me like he could just put the larger one sideways.

He held out his hand, palm up. I slapped it. He stared at me for a moment then started to laugh. It was a lovely, open-mouthed laugh, free and fearless. "I need the key! You're funny, Sally!"

I didn't bother correcting him. I got the key from the kitchen and opened the car remotely. He lifted the first box like it was packed with feathers. He slid it into the Prius's trunk. The car sighed.

"Uh, Sal? Did your car just complain?" His eyes were wide.

"Ignore it. It's a fussbudget."

"Does that mean *haunted*?"

"No, it means picky and grumpy."

"Ooh. Ok. *Fussbudget. Fussbudget.* Here's your second box, fussbudget!" He was right; only two would fit. "Where are you taking the boxes?"

"I'm going to get a storage unit at the other end of town."

"I can take the third box in my—oof! Did you put more books in here? It's even heavier than when I moved it yesterday."

"No, I didn't touch it. It's full, that's all. Just books.

"What about the big chair? That go too?"

"No, not yet. I may find a way to use it. Just the third box and we're good."

With some effort August loaded the third box into the bed of his truck. "Heavier than yesterday, that's for sure. Like I said, I know my boxes."

★ ★ ★

The storage place at the end of town had a big unit available, and a much smaller one, the disadvantage of the smaller one being that it was at the very far end of the facility. "We have dollies, if you need one," the woman who gave me the forms said. "Which one do you want?" I took the smaller one.

She moved her huge bulk to the side to reach the form drawer. I filled one out and gave her my credit card. "Oh, you're the new Keeper," she said.

I just nodded. There was no point.

"Here's your number. You need your own lock. Don't forget you have forty-eight hours to add us to your insurance policy as additionals, otherwise we cancel you."

"Lock?"

She gestured with one of her chins. "You can buy one, but that's cash only."

I fished in my handbag for some bills and bought a lock.

"Where are we going, Sal?" August said. He was practicing using my name right.

"Oh, August, I didn't see you there," the office woman said. "You helping Mrs. DeVine?"

"Nah, Mrs. Cochrane. I'm helping Sal."

"Don't go blasting that horn of yours, August, or I'm gonna tell your ma."

We headed over to the cars, me pulling a racketing dolly with one twisted wheel. "Looks like everyone knows everyone here," I said. He put the three boxes on the dolly.

"Oh yeah," August said. "Well, most of us, anyway. Not the real rich people. We know who they are but they don't know us." From the mouths of babes and innocents. "And some of the guys who don't speak English yet, they don't know us, but their kids do."

"The woman at the counter there knew who I was, and she knows your mom."

August grinned. "Yep. She used to teach fourth and fifth grade, till she couldn't stand it anymore. And she used to be in the pageant, like my Ma and Carinna. That's why they call her the White Lady."

"Wait what?"

"My Ma used to play an angel in the Christmas pageant in

the park, and she would dress all in white. Carinna did too. And Mrs. Cochrane was supposed to be the innkeeper, you know, the one that finally lets Mary and Joseph have the baby Jesus in the barn. But my mom fell a couple of years ago on some of the straw they put out for the Baby, and broke her scrotum, and couldn't be in the—what? Why are you laughing?"

I shook my head. "Sorry. Just trying to—ladies don't have scrotums—"

He blushed. "Shit. Oh, sorry, Sal. Oh man. What's the word. Her sputum?"

We were at the unit.

I opened it, and August moved the boxes in and locked the door.

"Where to next?"

"I'm going to take a drive. But why don't you go get yourself a nice snack? Or bring your mom a coffee and donut?" I took a twenty from my purse.

"You don't have to pay me, Sal. Your mom was real good to my Ma when she broke her . . . thing. In her back. From falling."

"Oh! Sacrum! No, I'm not paying you, just treating you to a snack. Here."

He took the twenty. "Thanks. My Ma will enjoy a treat. She isn't half as big as Mrs. Cochrane, but she can really put away a box of donuts!"

I was probably imagining it, but it looked like the Prius was sneering at me. "Jealous of that big, strong pickup truck?" I asked it.

★ ★ ★

The road wove between acres of vineyards, most just budding, some still no more than sentries with outstretched arms waiting for the right time to sprout. After a mile of flat land outside the eastern border of the town, the county changed. That was one of the strange things about Simpato. Well, one of the many other strange things. It sat at the nexus of three separate counties. Technically, it was in Valley County, but at the west and north it was in two others. One county was known for its beautiful coastline and fine wines; one was the meth capital of the state. Which, given California's population, was quite an honor.

The landscape hadn't changed yet, but the quality of the roadway had immediately deteriorated. Soon, the vineyards looked sparser and less well-tended, and then the road started to climb. I realized that I was not far from where I'd been yesterday, just approaching it from the other side of town.

The vegetation grew shrubby and wild, and I could see in the distance the pathway where we had walked. Down below, Simpato Lake and the irrigation holding-pond glittered blue. Ahead, the road climbed steeply, and soon I was well into Mount Santabella. It was drier up here, and I could glimpse dark spots where caves had been dug into the side of the mountain. I shivered.

Eventually, the road veered around to the far side of the mountain without going over the crest, and I was on the eastern slope. A sign for Cragstown said two miles. So it was that close.

To my right the land was more level, though ahead and to my left it still rose sharply. The meadow that extended southward had some light green grass, a few shrubs, and story poles, those long metal poles that showed where buildings would go. This had to be the location of a future development.

There was also a tall pine tree, right by the side of the road, unnaturally uniform in color and shape—a cell tower. As the cop had pointed out, there had been a similar tree where Carinna and I had been walking. Why did she say there was no reception then? Officer Aureliano had found that strange, given his sarcastic comment. Maybe the tower was new, and she didn't know that cell phones could work there now.

I pulled over to look at the developer's sign. "Pathways Development. Bringing housing to California where it's most needed." A nice sentiment. Odd that the nuns at the Little Sisters were opposed to it. Of course, they *were* the Little Sisters of the *Earth*. But wasn't housing one of the basic things that nuns were in favor of?

There didn't seem to be anything else nearby, so maybe the objection that there were no services or transportation near the development had some merit. It was much closer to Cragstown than Simpato, so it was surprising that it generated so much angst in Simpato. I recalled that someone had said that the mayor of Cragstown was happy to have the development. Since we were less than two miles from there, it would be more in his backyard than Simpato's. Unless there was something special about this meadow. Or the money was flowing the wrong way. Or it was a different project altogether. Very confusing.

I wondered who owned Pathways Development. It would be easy enough to check the Secretary of State website to see what kind of filing they had, what their tax-compliance status was, who their officers were, but it would be harder to look behind the curtain to who was controlling it financially.

I pulled back onto the road, and in a couple of minutes the first signs of Cragstown appeared. A run-down gas station, a couple of auto-repair shops, a bar. A bodega or minimart, another few stores, a stoplight. Two men started across the street, and a pickup going the opposite direction screeched to a stop. The two men turned and ran back, diving into a Mexican restaurant as the horn blared. A man with long brown hair came out of the car-repair shop and yelled a juicy obscenity at the truck. I ducked down in my seat, terrified that a shot would be fired, but the tires squealed and the pickup left, leaving the smell of tires in the air.

My heart was pounding. The light turned green and I inched forward, then sped up. This wasn't anywhere I wanted to be. I looked for a place to turn around, but didn't see one and made a right, figuring to go around the block and head back where I'd come from.

This block had houses and a couple of apartment buildings, not bad-looking, fairly well-kept. No one was on the street.

I made another right, and everything changed. Two burnt-out buildings stood empty, and the next lot had garbage and old household goods piled in a mountain next to a rusted car. A man with a shopping cart was vomiting at the curb. A knot of men at the corner were engrossed in something they were all looking at, and when I turned my third right I could see it was a little dog, lying on its side on the sidewalk. I couldn't tell if it was dead.

I returned to the main street, turned left, and headed back toward Simpato.

★ ★ ★

As I approached the development, I pulled to a stop. Police cars blocked the road, and an officer indicated I should turn left. I didn't want to. I didn't have any idea where that road would take me, but I sure as hell didn't want to go back to Cragstown. I lowered my window to explain. The cop put his hand on his hip.

I took my hands off the wheel and held them where he could see them. He walked toward me cautiously, nervous even though I was a little, middle-aged, white lady in a Prius. I didn't fool myself. I knew that each one of those descriptors mattered.

"If I turn left here, how do I get back to Simpato?" I asked.

"Make your first right, about three-quarters of a mile down this road, and it will put you right there."

I thanked him. "What's going on?" I asked. I hadn't heard sirens, but I supposed an accident could have happened in the five minutes I'd spent enjoying Cragstown.

He shook his head. "Move along."

I moved along.

I was now on the back side of the development, and I could

see that it stretched north toward Cragstown. I turned at the first right, as instructed, and the road narrowed to barely two lanes, with no shoulder, and dropped precipitously. I could see why the other road was the preferred route to Cragstown, though this road delivered me in ten minutes to Peaches Road, not a mile from my house. Cragstown was a lot closer than I'd thought.

★ ★ ★

When I got home there was a Simpato Police car parked outside my door. I pulled into the back, where the driveway and parking gravel were, and was less astonished than I'd like to think I would be to see both Officer Aureliano and Chief Plata sitting comfortably in my Brown Jordan lawn chairs on my deck. At least they had the decency to stand up when I got out of the car.

"Afternoon, Mrs. DeVine," Aureliano said. Too much work to correct him to Ms. I let it slide.

"Good afternoon, gentlemen. To what do I owe this visit?"

I was careful not to sound defensive or angry, but I didn't like it one bit that they felt free to come on my property and sit in my chairs. They both waited for me on the deck, not moving down to the driveway. I stopped at the top stair and waited for an answer.

Chief Plata stepped toward me. I hadn't realized what a physical presence he was when we were seated at the table in the station, but now, up close, he was formidable. On a different day that would be very interesting in a good, if academic, way, but today it felt excessive.

I'm a lawyer, I reminded myself. I know how to act around cops. I folded my arms, made my stance relaxed, and waited. Plata blinked. "We had some follow-up questions and thought we'd save you the trip. Would you like to sit out here or should we go inside?"

Would I like to have this interview with everyone on the street looking covertly through their windows? Or would I grant permission for them to enter my home?

"Come on in," I said. "I'll make coffee, though it won't be as good as the espresso you brought me at the station."

"Glad you liked it. Sergio's dad, that's Officer Gallego, the young guy, his dad runs the roastery in town, so he brings us the good stuff."

"I'll have to buy my coffee at the roastery from now on," I said. I put a K cup in the machine and put a mug beneath it. "Back in a flash."

"Where you going?" Aureliano said, tensing.

"To pee. This is my house, remember?"

Plata smiled a tiny bit. I walked past them. "Have a seat in the living room," I said. "Coffee will be ready in a minute."

When I came back, Chief Plata had a steaming mug in his hands, and Aureliano was standing at the little table, looking down at the box of cookies from the monastery. "Offering refreshments?" he said.

"Right. Have the cops buzzed while zooming around town." I made a second cup of coffee and offered it to Aureliano. "Milk? Sugar?"

"You have that pink sweetener?" Aureliano asked. I was getting pretty sick of him.

"No. Just sugar."

"Never mind, then, I'm sweet enough."

I hadn't heard that since high school. I made a third cup for myself, and Chief Plata pulled one of the two folding chairs at the table over to the folding and plush chairs in the center. I took the plush one, even though the folding chairs were more comfortable. This way they wouldn't have to do any rank pulling.

Aureliano pulled out his notepad, and so did the chief. "No recorder, so we'll have to take notes."

I shrugged.

"So, off taking a drive?" Chief Plata said casually.

"Yes." I wasn't fooled. But what did it matter? "I went to the storage unit and then drove up to where the development is going to be. Turned around in Cragstown, and came home. Why?"

"What time were you in Cragstown?"

I looked at my watch. "Not more than twenty minutes ago. Again, why?"

"No reason," Aureliano started.

"It's okay, Luke. Sal, we're trying to patch a few more things together, and something's come up. Let us ask you a few more questions, to pinpoint some times, and then we'll answer your questions, okay?"

Now we knew who the good cop was. But all I did was find the poor woman who was killed. And not even find her. All I did was stand near her while Carinna called the cops! Why am I feeling like I'm in trouble? Maybe everyone felt that way around police.

"Okay, but really, I want to understand why I'm being asked my whereabouts for a drive. So ask your questions, and I'll do my best to answer them, but I told you all I know yesterday."

Chief Plata put his cup on the floor. "I know. It's awful. You find a poor woman in the mountain, and next thing you're being asked a ton of questions. But we just need to know some things. So, let's go over the visit to the monastery again. Who was there? At the service."

I closed my eyes. "The nuns, of course . . ."

"Which ones did you recognize?"

"Only Sister Sorghum, because she came here and gave me those cookies, and I met Mother Sassafras when I walked in. Then, someone spoke, Sister Calendula, and then one of the younger nuns, Marigold," I stifled an eyeroll, "Sister Marigold asked to speak with me after the service. She also questioned my trustworthiness to be the new Keeper. Which, by the way, was something I had no intention of being. And now it seems that I am, whether I want to be or not."

"Yeah," the chief said. "We'll get to that. So, who else do you remember seeing?"

"Carinna was sitting behind me. Two teen-aged girls, no more than fifteen, were giggling in a row in the back. Three or four—I can't remember—older grandmother types. And up in the balcony, the mayor and someone I was told is named Scooter, the librarian. In the back, alone, a tall red-haired woman with big features. Carinna told me that was Georgiana Noyes, the woman that writes—wrote—died, um the gossip columnist. Carinna made a little joke about how we all were going to be in the column this coming week because we were all here. And the mayor was supposed to speak. But he left—I told you this part already."

"Did you try any of the cookies? Or any food at all?"

"Food? They only offered cookies. And I knew better than to try any cookies. I figured that out after Sister Sorghum dropped those two off. I don't do cannabis."

"It's legal," Aureliano said. "And they have a permit to sell them."

"So?" I said. "Still not my thing."

"Okay," Chief Plata said. "That's the timeline. And you didn't eat or drink anything there."

"Nope."

"When you first saw Ms. Noyes, Georgiana, you didn't know if she was dead. Why not?"

"Because I have no experience with dead people? How would I know? I put my hand on her, she wasn't wearing a shirt, and her skin was cool, but not cold. It just felt, I don't know, dead. But either way I knew that help was on the way, so I told her that."

"And when did the mayor leave?"

"What? You mean the service?" Plata nodded. "I don't know. I looked up and they were gone."

"Okay, one last thing. What happened to the boxes that were on your deck this morning?"

I stared at him. "Chief," I started.

"Please. Devon."

"Devon, that's a weird and disturbing question. I'll answer it, but this is a strange thing to ask me. I took them to storage. With August's help."

Everyone sat quietly for a moment. "Mind if we go over there with you? Take a look inside the boxes?"

I frowned. "Are you kidding?"

He shook his head. "No. I'm not. Something odd is going on."

"Besides a prominent person in your community being killed?" I said.

"Killed? What makes you think someone was killed?"

"What is this, the Twilight Zone?"

Devon pursed his lips, but Luke Aureliano clearly missed the reference.

"We don't know if Georgiana was killed or not. We know she's dead, that's all."

"Given the way her forehead was bashed, I'd say it was obvious. Most women don't go around taking their blouses off on a relatively cool Spring day and then lying down in a little cave and bashing their own head in. Just because."

"Have you talked to Carinna since yesterday?" Devon asked, ignoring my outburst.

I shook my head no.

Chief Plata—Devon—stood up. Aureliano followed suit. "Sal, I'm going to check a few things, and then I'd like you to come to the station first thing in the morning tomorrow. Say, nine thirty or ten. We should know a lot more by then. Meanwhile, here's my cell phone. If you think of anything at all, call me. Anything. Can you do that?"

"Sure." I programmed his number into my phone. He did the same with mine.

"And if you see Carinna, or Scooter, or the mayor, I want you to call me right away. Okay?"

I nodded, but that was more reflex than agreement. Why would I want to do that? "Are they missing or something?"

"Or something," Aureliano said.

"See you tomorrow," Chief Plata said. I opened the door for them and watched them walk the long path to their car on the street. I was really going to have to get a fence.

★ ★ ★

"Has anyone seen Mayor Solis?"

That was the lead on Facebook's Without a Duck page. Some local business owners who were tired of the infighting and backbiting of some of the other sites had started the page, with participation and membership by invitation only. The page was affectionately known as the WAD.

I was delighted to find an invitation in my inbox from, oddly enough, an old lawyer-friend of my dad's from years ago. I wasn't much of a social-media user, I'd told him, sounding like everyone else I knew who was addicted to the thing. But even ten years ago, we'd all been playing around with it, and it had aged right along with us. This old pal had to be seventy-five if he was a day, had been a lawyer in Sacramento like my dad, and also had a house near Simpato, but close to the river. He and his wife had retired there around the time my folks had moved to live here full-time, but I'd never thought much about them.

I looked at his photo and teared up a little. That's about how my dad would have looked, if he'd still been around. Blond hair gone white, squinting blue eyes, a generous smile.

My dad had been taller, though, and had a long jawline that sometimes made him look like Ichabod Crane before his head fell off and was replaced by a pumpkin—Ichabod's, that is, not my dad's. His name brought a smile: Brooks Campbell, like the soup, he used to say. Scottish to my dad's Jewish, they used to exchange jokes about each other's ethnicities that would never be allowed today. And yet they knew each other as absolute and unwavering supporters.

A message accompanied the invite to the page: "Little Sal, I know that Stan would have been so happy to know that his follow-in-my-footsteps daughter had followed him to the house in Simpato. We're still here too, if you ever want to drop by. I know how busy you young people are. Catherine and I would love to see you. We miss Stan and Alta so much. And here's a nice page with plenty of Simpato news. I think you'll enjoy it!"

I sent him back a thank-you message, assured him that I was well, and clicked over to the WAD page. WADdle, WADdle, it said at the top. Of course.

"Has anyone seen Mayor Solis?"

The question was posted by someone whose profile picture was a duck holding a wine glass, and whose business name was PatoVino. I couldn't determine who was behind the business just by looking at it. The answers were few.

"Saw him three days ago at the liquor store ha ha"

"At the council meeting last Monday, where he and the Nose were gettin into it"

"Getting it on more likely"

"Inappropriate. Moderator should delete."

"Sorry, you're right. I should delete but I don't know how."

At that point the "inappropriate" comment had twenty likes, most of them laugh-faces.

Carinna had posted last: "Saw him at the LSOTE service. He left early. Maybe Scooter knows."

This was better than other sites? It was scurrilous, but it

gave me a way to contact Carinna. I looked at her page. Carinna Monarch. Decent photo. Background was her truck. I friend-requested her and was accepted within minutes. I messaged her: *What's your phone number. We need to talk.*

Once the formalities were accomplished, I texted Carinna. *Want to meet for a glass of wine? Strange doings today.*

She thumbs-up'd the message and suggested a spot not far from my house. *Really touristy, no one will know us there.*

An hour later we were at a little table looking out on Central Avenue, the principal commercial row of Simpato's downtown, holding extraordinarily expensive glasses of wine. Mine was white, a bit sweet, with an explosion of citrus and floral flavors that were unexpected but wholly in harmony. I could smell the earth-aroma of Carina's glass of red from two feet away. All in all, in the five days I'd been in Simpato I'd had five times as much wine as I would have had in San Francisco.

"What a nightmare," Carinna said. She stretched her long, meaty legs, encased in white stretch pants, below the table, colliding with the empty chair at the table next to us.

After I righted the chair, I nodded. "Not what I'd planned. Have you been okay?"

She shrugged. Her top, a long white tunic with gold sequins on the shoulders, caught the light as she moved and reflected in her shades. She pushed the sunglasses up on her head, and raised her glass.

As she sipped her wine, I took some time to look at her. Since that meeting in the Duck Shop parking lot, I hadn't really taken stock of her, besides the facts that she was tall, sturdy, and wore white. Now I saw that her green eyes were narrow and surrounded by lines and crows-feet, her complexion was fair, her hair was a darker brown than mine and, like mine, was threaded with gray. She wore it short, kind of a pixie cut, but the bangs had grown out into a shaggy fringe along the sides of her face.

"You live alone?" I ventured.

Again the shrug. "I do now. Was married for ten years, then had another guy for a few, but on my own now. Got a grown daughter, she lives up in the foothills, near Nevada City. She brews beer and grows cannabis. What about you?"

"Oh, you know. Married for almost twenty years, hubby played around plenty but was pretty cool otherwise, until he messed up at work." That covered a lot. "And the intern talked." Not exactly, but it made for a simpler tale. "I didn't really have a choice. We worked for the same firm, so everyone knew. He was the high-earner; I was the one who left."

Carinna shook her head sympathetically. "So you came home to your parents' old home to regroup."

"Yeah, lick my wounds, figure out my life. What about you? Besides being an angel in the local pageant, what do you do for work?"

She stared. "Look, I know everyone knows everything about everyone in this dump, but how did you know about the—wait. August, right?"

"Yep." She still hadn't told me how she earned a living and Simpato, while small, wasn't a cheap place to live. "You work here in town?"

She sipped her wine. "I help my daughter with her business," she said at last.

Ah. Code for *I sell pot.*

I wondered if she supplied the Little Sisters, for their cookies. No polite way to ask that, so I asked something else. "Tell me about Georgiana Noyes."

She smiled, but it wasn't a happy smile. "Gossip Nose? She didn't make a lot of friends here, I can tell you that."

"Enough friends to get herself elected to city council."

"True. I guess some folks liked her. Not many. She moved here about twenty years ago, so not a born-and-bred Original-Simpato-Highschool-Duck resident like I am. She used to write a tourist column for the weekly, called This Week in Simpato. You know, visit this winery, that boutique, so-and-so is having an amazing sale, don't miss it. That kind of boosterism stuff, so that was well-received. At least by those whose businesses she pumped."

I wondered if my mom knew her. She must have.

"Then the rumors started," Carinna continued. "Folks were saying that you had to pay her to get mentioned and, if that was the case, her This Week in Simpato was nothing more than glorified advertising, with the fees going straight to the writer. So she started another column, still doing the This Week column, but also added a Local News from the Nose. The paper loved her. Folks bought the paper the minute it came out, just to see if they were in The Nose. Dreading and hoping, I guess.

"After a bit, she changed This Week to add stuff from outside the town itself, stopped using a byline, and it became clearer that it really was advertising. The Nose column was so popular that she had a real following all through the county. That's one of the reasons the *Quack* is still in business, when all the papers are dying or dead."

The unspoken, as we sipped our wine, was *and now she's dead.*

CHAPTER SIX

Monday morning started with a text, and by nine a.m. I was swimming in information, questions, and demands.

I was awakened by Chief Plata's text: *Sal, can you get down to the station at ten? Devon.* This was followed by a surprise text from my sister, Dahlia, telling me to look at Facebook because the WAD page was saying stuff about Mom. So Dahlia knew about the WAD page, and probably about Mom having been the town's secret-keeper. I had to wonder how disconnected I had been.

The entire WAD post asking where the mayor was had been taken down. On the other hand, a post on the page announced that The New Keeper was going to start having hours and invited her to introduce herself and let everyone know when she'd be available. That gem had been posted by the WAD page moderator, also welcoming me to the page. I had to put a stop to that, or somehow get a handle on it.

A comment said: "I thought she said Tuesday."

"Cool. Anyone know what time?"

"Probably evening. IDK. If she's on, can you tell us?"

"God I miss our old Keeper. She was the most compassionate woman on the planet. I hope the New Keeper can live up to her."

"Not f-in likely"

"Moderator?"

I felt my pulse racing, not in a good way. More like *Flee! Flee!* in the fight-or-flight syndrome.

And then an email from Saul, asking if he and I could talk sometime soon, maybe today, about "everything." Given that the divorce was final, I couldn't imagine what kind of *everything* we'd be talking about, but in an abundance of caution I checked my bank accounts and my investment portfolio. All seemed in order. I had opened a completely separate brokerage account for my payoff settlement, at a different institution, so there was no chance of Saul screwing with it. Unlike the intern.

And lastly, a text from an unknown number: *This is Scott Hudson, the librarian. I got your number from Carinna. Would you like to have breakfast with me? Scooter.*

Where to begin?

The meeting with the police chief was a command, not a request, no matter how nicely phrased, so I simply texted back *yes* to Chief Plata. Devon my ass.

I reread the Facebook post. How could I post a giant NO! when this was something everyone was expecting? All the more reason to make it clear I wasn't stepping into my mother's role, whatever it had been. But it needed to be phrased carefully, especially if I was really going to be a resident here. And maybe even a lawyer here. I wished there was someone I could talk this through with.

I supposed I could text or call Dal, but she'd probably be ecstatic—maybe literally—that I was going to be the Keeper. Maybe she'd suggest a Tarot reading for me.

My friends from San Francisco would absolutely not understand. My two nonlawyer pals would just shake their heads, say that country living was mighty strange, and that it sounded like a gas to try being the town secrets keeper. My one real friend who hadn't deserted me after the humiliation of the suspension would say, "Who ever heard of such a thing? It sounds medieval. Just tell everyone that you're not ready to start, and then put it off until they forget about you."

As if it were that easy.

The email from Saul was the easiest to answer. "No, Saul. We're divorced." I hit *send.*

I read the one from Scooter again. Maybe if I could just call him Scott it might be less weird. Could I fit breakfast in before going to the police station? It would give the meal a good established end-time, so if it was awkward I could plead a summons from the authorities.

I texted, *Yes, but I have to be at the police station by 9:45. Tell me where.*

It was eight thirty now. If he didn't answer right away it would give me an easy out. My phone binged. *Nine at the Duck Bill? See you there.*

I shrugged. Time for a quick shower and some makeup. I hoped I was doing the right thing.

★ ★ ★

The Duck Bill was packed. Families with kids, elderly couples sharing a single order of French toast, three young women with smudges under their eyes getting a last breakfast in after a girls' weekend, tables of couples holding hands, and the counter lined with men, beefy or thin, with coffee and the *Quack,* talking back and forth like the long-time acquaintances they were.

Simpato High Ducks all.

I looked around for Scott/Scooter. He'd corralled a table in the far corner and had coffee already, as well as a folded copy of the *Quack.* He stood as I approached.

This was a librarian?

If Chief Devon Plata was muscular and manly, Scott/Scooter Hudson was a surfer-boy grown up. What I had seen of his hair at the monastery had been misleading, as it had been pulled back into a ponytail invisible from the front. Now it hung loose, golden-brown with streaks of blond that many women would pay their stylist big bucks to try to achieve, long enough to just brush his shoulders, tucked back behind his ears. A strand worked loose and dropped over his forehead as he leaned over to pull out my chair.

His hands were big and knuckley. His shoulders pulled against the white-and-light-blue striped collared shirt he wore open at the neck, his sleeves rolled up to show ropy forearms, and his jeans, faded blue to white, looked narrow like his long legs. He smiled, his blue eyes crinkled, his white teeth bright against his gold-burnished tan. How did I not notice all this at the monastery? All I saw then was a tall man looking at his phone and smirking at me.

All I saw now was the stand-in for a movie star.

"Salvia?" he said, shattering the dream. His voice was nearly as high as mine and almost a whisper.

We shook hands, and for a flash I thought, the hands make up for the voice.

Down girl!

I sat and a waitress in an old-fashioned, traditional waitress uniform—black dress, black apron, support hose—handed me a menu. I had an outfit like that once, I remembered. I worked summer after summer at a cafe near Sac State, as we called California State University at Sacramento, and we wore these throw-back uniforms that were retro twenty-five years ago. I looked quickly at the offerings, ordered a waffle and coffee, and turned back to the surfer-vision across from me.

"Welcome to Sin-Pato," he said.

"Thanks, Scott," I said, trying out his real name.

"Scooter, to most of the folks here in town," he rasped. "Remnant of fifth grade at Duckless Elementary." I laughed. *Duckless* was a new one.

"And that makes me Sal. To get away from my own fifth-grade nightmare, *Saliva*."

He grinned at me. Lordy, he was handsome. "So, you've moved back. Or not really back, but into your parents' house. What brings you home?"

"Not home, as you know. They bought this place after I was grown and married, so I only visited now and then. You've been here all your life?" I wanted to turn the conversation away from my past, remembering his smirk from the balcony of the monastery.

Scooter shook his head. "Nah. Almost, though. I went to UC Santa Barbara for college, got my Masters in Library Science there too, and was there until, well . . ." He lifted his chin. A thick scar ran right where the neck joined the jaw, under his chin. "Made a few mistakes in my life," he said. "After this one, I came back to Simpato to recover, and stayed."

"We all make mistakes," I said, and I hoped I didn't blush.

My waffle came right then, easing the awkwardness.

"We do," he answered. "You certainly did."

I leaned in, focusing on his raspy voice. It was hard to tell if it was accusatory or mocking or just an observation. I went with that.

"Yup. But I divorced the sucker." A way to work that in, while making it my mistake.

Didn't quite work.

"I'm a librarian," Scooter said. "I look stuff up. You're under suspension from the State Bar, and the accusation was fraud. So's your, what, ex-husband Saul? He got two years; you got two months. So I figure you were swept up in something he masterminded. Am I right?"

"Why did you want to meet with me this morning?" I said in my best lawyer voice.

"Am I right?" he asked again.

"You're missing a few pieces your google search didn't turn

up. So let's hear about your mistake, huh?" I was mad, and defensive.

He leaned back, and I had to really concentrate to hear him. "I show you mine and you show me yours? Is that how you work?"

It wasn't sexy.

I shook my head. "You invite me to breakfast. You tell me why. *That's* how I work."

He sighed. "Sorry. I think we got off on the wrong foot, which surprises me, because that's not what I intended. That happens sometimes, because I can't make my voice convey the emotion I'm trying to express."

I didn't say, *going for the disabled-sympathy vote.*

"Words do a pretty good job of conveying what folks are trying to communicate, even in a monotone," I did say.

"Harsh."

"Yes, I can be. But Scott," I dispensed with the *Scooter* business, "if you want to know what happened to me, you'll need to tell me why you're asking. I have no real need to know what happened to your throat and, since I barely know you, I can't say I'm burning up with curiosity. And as far as I can tell, you have zero need to know what went down with the State Bar. Unlike you, most people aren't going to try to find out, so unless you're into something crude and ineffective like blackmail, you need to tell me why you want to know. Now, I've got to get to the police station, so here's a twenty to cover my share of the breakfast." I put a bill on the table and stood up. "I'm happy to talk to you, but a little honesty goes a real long way."

"Honesty, huh?"

I walked out.

★ ★ ★

Chief Plata was on a call, so Sergio, the very young cop— the closer I got the younger he seemed—brought me a cup of their delicious coffee. Since I'd left my coffee undrunk and my emotions raw at the Duck Bill, it was a welcome nerve-steadier.

I thought through the odd conversation with the librarian. Such a handsome man, such a shame. He had been looking me up when he caught my eye at the monastery. I hadn't imagined it. And that was something he wanted to know more about. I had no idea why.

Perhaps I could have handled that better, I thought now.

I looked up when Luke Aureliano came through the door leading back from the reception area into the depths of the police station. Behind him, and now passing in front of him as he held the door open, were the two teenaged girls who had been at the service. "Bye, Luke," one said. "Tell Lucy I'm coming over to see the baby!"

"You come over, you babysit!" he said. The two girls giggled as one.

He was still holding the door, and now a middle-aged woman with a scarf over her graying hair came out. "*Gracias, Señora*," Aureliano said.

She nodded and answered in Spanish. "I don't like my girls being involved in any police business."

"They were very helpful," he said, in English.

"Celia! Celia and Mercedes! Don't you hurry away. We're going straight home!" she said, again in Spanish.

The girls turned around, rolling their eyes at Aureliano. "See what trouble you got us into, Luke? Now we're not going to get to go anywhere!" the first one said.

"Yeah, thanks a lot!" the second one said, and punched him in the arm.

"Hey, Mercedes! You gonna get arrested if you hit a cop!" Aureliano said.

The girls laughed, and one held the door for their mother.

At that moment, Chief Plata came out. The girls scurried out the door quickly, and their mother glanced back at Aureliano. He nodded and turned to his chief.

"A word?"

Chief Plata nodded. "Sal, give me a minute here. Sergio, did you get Mrs. DeVine coffee?"

"He did," I answered for him.

"Good. I'll be with you in a second."

He and Aureliano passed back into the inner area, and the door clicked shut. I realized that it was locked from inside. "Can I use the ladies' room?" I asked Sergio, who had sat back behind the desk that surveyed the reception area. He had stood when the chief had come out, but I also realized that the young girls hadn't even glanced at him.

Probably something else left over from middle school.

"Um, it's inside," he said. "Maybe you should wait until the chief comes back out."

I nodded. He had all the authority of a gnat.

★ ★ ★

Fortunately, it was only a few minutes before the door opened. "The chief is ready for you," Aureliano said.

"She wants to use the bathroom," Sergio volunteered. No wonder the girls ignored him. His social skills at twenty-two or twenty-four or whatever he was had to have improved from what they'd been in high school, after the police academy and all. They were tragic.

"Of course," Aureliano said. "This way, please." He held the door. "Over here, past the drinking fountain. And the chief's office is the next one across the hall, when you're ready."

As I entered the restroom I heard him say to Sergio, "*Pendejo.* If a witness wants to go to the bathroom you let them, okay? We serve the public, *tonto.*"

Poor Sergio.

When I'd finished, I went back into the hall, and knocked lightly on Chief Plata's open door. He smiled. "Come on in," he said. "Shut the door behind you."

So this was to be a private conversation. No recording, no Officer Luke Aureliano, no witnesses.

I sat down.

"Thanks for coming in," he said. "As you can see, this is a conversation between me and you. Unless you don't want it to be, in which case I'll ask Luke to sit in."

Once again, I had a choice of how to respond. I wasn't going to make the same mistake twice. "Let me hear you out. If I feel uncomfortable, I'll ask for the formalities. Is that okay?"

The chief smiled a bit. "Interesting. Okay, sounds good. But I'm hoping to do more listening than talking. So, Sal, here's the issue. When did you last see the mayor?"

"I told you yesterday. The first and only time I ever saw the man I was told was the mayor—I've never met him; I have no actual knowledge about him—was at the monastery during their service. I was told, the nun giving a report, her name was Calendula, said he'd be speaking to everyone about the development. Everyone looked up at the balcony, and he stood there with the man I now know is Scott Hudson, called Scooter, who's the librarian, but I didn't know that then. I saw them up there during the service, they were there through most of it, but by the end they were both gone. That's the only time I've ever seen him."

"You sure?"

"Yes! What's this about?"

"And when was the last time you saw Scooter?"

"Fifteen minutes ago."

"What?!"

"He invited me to breakfast. We had a short breakfast at the Duck Bill. I met him there at about nine fifteen, and left there at about nine forty to come here."

He looked at his watch. I didn't look at mine, but I knew it was about ten after ten, as I had been right on time, and the business with the girls and the bathroom had burned up about ten minutes.

He picked up the phone. "Sergio, tell Aureliano to get in here."

"What's going on, Chief Plata?"

"Devon. Really. I'm not actually sure."

Aureliano came into the room without knocking. "Yeah, Chief? Want me to sit in after all?"

Plata shook his head. "No. Hop on over to the Duck Bill, see if Scooter's still there. If he is, tell him I need to see him. Pronto. And if he's not there, he'll be at the library."

"Okay, boss."

As soon as he was gone, Plata leaned back in his chair. "I might as well tell you, because it will be all over town in about an hour. No one has seen Sebastian Solis, the mayor, since you did. At least that's what everyone is saying. And you are the only one who's said that he was on the balcony with Scooter. No one else has mentioned the librarian at all. The mayor's not at home, he's not in his office—he's an offsite sales rep for a feed company when he isn't mayoring—no one has seen him anywhere. He didn't keep his appointment to speak to the nuns, he didn't go to Mass yesterday and, no matter whether he's a believer or not, the mayor of Simpato goes to Sunday Mass."

So he took a little breather from the overwhelming intrusiveness of this little town? But I didn't say that, because that wasn't what Plata—I'd work up to Devon eventually—wanted to hear.

"And on Sunday," the chief took a deep breath, "while you were exploring Cragstown, it looks like he left his car, crosswise across the lanes, on the road going past the development."

Ah.

We were quiet for a moment. "So that's why the police turned me aside to that other road," I said finally.

"Yeah. And some poor old lady was coming down from Cragstown, maybe a little faster than she ought to have, and hit his car broadside. Poor gal. She wasn't hurt, just shook up. She spent the night over at the hospital, but she swears the car was empty when she hit it."

"But I had come that way not ten minutes earlier and there was no one there. I even pulled over . . ."

He waited. Now I understood why he wanted to talk to me.

"I forgot that part yesterday. I didn't even think of it. I pulled over to read the developer's sign, look at the story poles. I was there for maybe five minutes, probably less. Then I continued up to Cragstown, which was really unpleasant—"

"Not Simpato, that's for sure. Did you see anything at all when you were there that you can tell us?"

I shook my head. "Only that two guys were crossing the street when a pickup truck came barreling down the road and squealed to a stop, then the two guys ran back the way they'd come and dove into a storefront of a Mexican restaurant. I ducked down, I was at the light, I was afraid there would be shooting, but the pickup just burned some rubber and left."

"Tell me everything you can remember about the truck." He picked up the phone again, swore, and put it down. "Hold on." He picked the phone up again and said, "Sergio, bring a recorder and a notepad. You're going to witness your first statement in a murder case."

"Murder case?"

"Georgiana Noyes, remember?"

"But yesterday you said she wasn't murdered!"

"Now I think differently, but keep it under your hat. In fact, that was what I wanted to talk to you about in the first place. About the Keeper. But—"

Sergio came in, clearly excited. He sat down next to me. "Here, Chief?"

Plata nodded. "Turn the recorder on, state your name, mine, and Mrs. DeVine's and then the date and time."

I watched Sergio do as he was told, his fingers shaking.

"Now, Mrs. DeVine, tell me everything you can remember about the truck you saw in Cragstown."

I went through the whole thing again. Going to the storage unit. Deciding to go for a drive, heading to Cragstown. Getting to Cragstown.

He asked me the color—black—; the make—I didn't know—; the license plate—ditto—; to describe the driver—I couldn't, but I did my best with the two men running out and back.

"Oh, and some guy came out of the car repair shop near the corner and swore at them." He made me describe that man too.

He took me through time, the turns I made to turn around, my speed—slow—and my reasons for going there in the first place. "But I was only there for about five minutes. How could any of those guys have done anything two or three miles down the road?"

"We just need to cover all the bases," he said. "You're the common denominator in each of these events." I startled. "No, relax, I'm not saying you had anything to do with them; it's just that you seem to have been there each time. That's all."

Unspoken was, *and that's plenty.*

When we were done, he asked Sergio if he had any questions for me. "Just one, Chief." Plata nodded. "Mrs. DeVine, how come you took the boxes to storage yesterday?"

"Because I didn't need the stuff in them."

He glanced at Plata again. "But that could have waited until Monday, right? Were you in a hurry?"

I shook my head. "No, but August offered to help, and I guess he works during the week, so it was convenient."

"August says one of the boxes was heavier than it was the day before," he insisted. Plata sat up straighter. Sergio continued, "I hang out with him sometimes, we go to the bars in Cragstown, get some beers. He told me. It's bothering him."

Plata looked over at me. "He mentioned that to me," I agreed. "But I thought nothing of it."

"And it probably is nothing," Plata said. "Thanks, Sergio, you're excused."

Sergio got up, handing the recorder to Plata.

When he was gone, Plata turned to me. "Why didn't you tell me yesterday?"

"I don't know. None of that seemed particularly relevant, to the point where I didn't even think about telling you or not."

He nodded. "I should have told you about the mayor's car," he said. "You might have realized earlier. We've lost a day, but that can't be helped now."

"Where do you think he is?" I asked. "The mayor?"

"Out on the mountain somewhere, maybe."

"Like camping?" I asked.

"Like dead."

★ ★ ★

Now that I had Carinna's number, I texted her to go walking with me. But not around No Duck Lake, not this time. *Anywhere else that's good?*

She suggested the Long Vine Path, which ran from Simpato to Valley.

The bike path? I asked. That had been there back when my folks lived here.

It's way better now, she texted back.

I went home to get changed, and by then it was time for lunch. I opened my cabinets, newly stocked with nothing for lunch. I had a bowl of cereal. The waffle I'd left uneaten on my plate at the Duck Bill sure would have been good right then.

I went over the information I'd gotten and given this morning. It was a lot to digest on a nearly empty stomach. Before I even thought about it, I'd opened the box of cookies and taken a bite. I spat it out. It tasted vile. Of course. I'd forgotten somehow.

I tossed the box in the recycling.

I took out a notepad, the yellow pads all lawyers favor, and made a list of everything that had happened. No wonder folks had abandoned notepads for computers. I kept having to put other matters I remembered into the list, with arrows to where they actually belonged. I took out my laptop and typed it into a document, more orderly now. I added a few more things once I could insert items without arrows and writing up the side of the page.

Wednesday, April 7

I move in

August drives by, honks and waves

Thursday, April 8

I go to Duck Shop, meet Carinna

I read the Quack, where I'm mentioned. So's the mayor. Not in a nice way, by Georgiana, and in letters to the editor.

Friday April 9

Sister Sorghum stops by, leaves cookies (now stale, now in trash, turn out to be pot-laced.) She invites me to the monastery.

August stops by, makes himself comfortable on my lawn furniture

Saturday, April 10

Raining

August pushes my boxes under the eaves

Visit monastery, attend "service"

Meet nuns

Go walking with Carinna

Find dead Georgiana

Puke

Carinna goes down to call cops

Cops come

Sergio pukes

Get interviewed by cops: Luke Aureliano, Devon Plata Chief. Have wine with Carinna. Find out her daughter grows cannabis. Is that important? IDK

Was that all on one day? No wonder Saturday felt like an eternity.

Sunday, April 11

August comes over and helps take boxes to storage. Says one's heavier than before. Pay no attention.

Go to storage.

Drive up to Cragstown on the Cragstown Road. See development location, with story poles where the buildings will go. See three or four blocks of Cragstown, including menacing pickup truck and men, crowd of down-and-outers on corner with dog, come back down Cragstown Road.

Redirected to side road that turns into Peaches Drive near where we walked.

Cops on the deck ask more questions

Monday—today

Breakfast with Scooter Hudson librarian. Does not go well. He knows about my suspension.

More interview with Plata, then Sergio ___ (what's his last name) asks about boxes.

Plata and Aureliano asked about the boxes on Sunday. What's with the boxes?

Learn that Mayor Solis might be—dead

Learn that his car was on the Cragstown Road which was why I got rerouted.

★ ★ ★

I looked over the list. A few things were still missing. Like all the different nuns at the monastery, all against the development. Like Marigold and the other young one also not trusting the mayor, who was there with the librarian. And that the mayor, the librarian, the councilwoman/gossip columnist, a couple of teenaged girls, a few older ladies, and Carinna were all at that "service."

That the mayor of Cragstown was happy about the development.

I shook my head to clear the cobwebs. None of this made any sense at all, and if I hadn't found the poor woman with Carinna I would have absolutely no idea any of this was going on.

Or would I? Georgiana Noyes couldn't write about it in the *Quack*, since she was dead. Who would have written—wait a minute.

I quickly went to google. Today's issue of the *Quack* was already out, I knew that because half the people at the Duck Bill had copies they were reading with their breakfast, including Scooter the librarian.

But today's issue wasn't up on their site yet. I wondered if that was to encourage purchase. I needed a copy. I needed to see what the paper said about the death of their popular correspondent.

I went to Facebook to find the WAD page.

There was a photo of Georgiana, outlined in black. "Rest in Power" it said, so overused and only applicable to a few, like Ruth Bader Ginsberg, but now thrown around all over. This notice only gave the dates.

But the comments were what I really needed.

"Stuck her Nose one place too many!" said someone who went by BBBest.

"She'll be missed!" by most.

"How did she die?" someone asked.

"She fell, hiking on Mount Santabella. People need to be more careful."

"Don't judge."

"Not judging. But folks think it's like taking a walk in the park instead of respecting the mountain."

"That's judging!"

"No. You're not the policeman of the internet, so MYOB."

"STFU, bee-ach."

"Moderator? You on?"

Okay, that disintegrated fast. All was well in Simpato, until either it wasn't or until folks got on the internet.

So, word that she'd been murdered, or that at least Plata thought she had been, hadn't made it out of the police station yet. It wouldn't be long, not with a couple of teenagers being interviewed. Then I caught myself. Like the post said, *Don't judge*. After all, the people being most ugly and gossipy were the adults.

CHAPTER SEVEN

Carinna and I met at the trail. It really had been improved since Saul and I had walked it at least a decade ago, on our visits to my folks. It used to be a narrow, hard-dirt trail, mostly for bikes, and became a sodden mud-mess when it rained. Hikers walked it at their peril, but it wove charmingly between vineyards all the way to Valley.

Now it was about ten feet wide, paved, and had a walking side and a bike side. It still wound its way among the vines, and though it had rained on Saturday, it was dry and pleasant walking. The vines were budding almost as we watched.

I took a deep breath of earth-scented air. Glorious, especially after the past few days.

"Nice, huh?" Carinna said. "And to think they want to rip this all out for the development."

"Here? There's a development going in here too?"

"Here's where the development everyone's talking about is going."

"What? No! I drove over to the development yesterday, it's up near Cragstown!"

Carinna turned to face me. "My dear, you have been seriously misinformed."

"No, I'm not. It's about two miles before Cragstown. Pathways Development, right?"

She frowned. We walked a bit. "Yeah, that's the name. But the plan is to put it more or less here. It's been before the city council about twelve times in the past year and a half. We've had meetings and protests and everything else."

"Then where are the signs? And the story-poles showing where the buildings are going to go?"

"What are you talking about?"

We walked a little farther.

"This is nuts, Carinna. I drove up to Cragstown on Sunday, passed the site of the proposed development, pulled over, looked at the sign, and then left. And you're telling me that's not the development that everyone's talking about?"

"I don't know, Sal. I've not heard of one outside Cragstown. Toward Simpato, you say?"

"Yeah. I never got more than about three blocks into Cragstown before I turned around. And when I was heading back, I was redirected onto a side road that led me to Peaches Avenue. Plus," I said, "I told Chief Plata—"

"Who?"

"Devon Plata, the chief of police."

"Oh, Devon. No one calls him Chief Plata."

"Okay. Anyway, I told him about my drive, and he never said anything about not being the *right* development."

"This is really strange," Carinna said. "Turn around here?"

We walked silently for a bit. "Carinna, when was the last time the development was debated at the city council?"

She thought for a while. "About six months ago. After that, nothing except a few barbs in the paper and online. I thought they were revising their proposal and that was why everything went quiet. Until the service at the monastery."

"Did you know that was going to be talked about at the service? I mean ahead of time? Or do you go often?"

She chuckled. "I'm a pretty vital part of their economy."

As I suspected. But that didn't answer my question. I asked again. "So you knew the topic for this past weekend, since you're pretty involved?"

She nodded. "Sister Calendula put the word out that the mayor had some important announcements about the development, and that, well, that you were back. So I went, and some other folks went."

"Did you know what the mayor was going to announce?"

She shook her head. "I think even Calendula and Sorghum were in the dark. Some huge announcement, and we were going to hear it before anyone else. That sort of thing. But I didn't have any idea what."

I would have to ask those nuns, for sure.

"Why did those teenagers go? Are they young climate-change activists?" Saving the earth, if possible, was going to happen through the young's efforts.

She laughed. "No, it's the cookies. The monastery isn't supposed to allow anyone under 18, but the teens make a big fuss about the ecology, as you guessed, and then sneak cookies."

I thought about their exit from the police station, accompanied by their disapproving mother. Kids.

After a bit, I had another question. "Let's assume that Georgiana didn't take off her blouse all by herself, then trip and fall into a cave. Has there ever been anyone else killed, I mean, you know, murdered, in Simpato?"

Carinna looked into the distance. "Yeah. When your folks were still here. It was crazy. There was a really smarmy guy, he sold real estate, I think. And he was found hog-tied and drowned in Valley River. He had an Italian last name, so everyone figured it was Mafia related, though we'd never had any Mafia activity here before. I mean, there's no crime in Simpato."

"Did they catch who did it?"

She shook her head. "The worst thing was that poor August

found him. He's not quite right, you know, and poor guy was so upset. I mean, anyone would be, right? But he just went unhinged. And the prior police chief, the one before Devon, had August arrested. I mean, really. And accused him of murdering that guy. I wish I could remember his name. Obviously, they realized the mistake, let poor August go, and fired the chief. Gave him a fat pension, though. After that, for a bit we just had Sheriff's Deputies, no chief. Then Devon came."

"Was Devon a born-and-bred resident?"

"You mean an Original Duck? No. He came from Oregon or something. But he's been part of the community ever since. Good guy, I think."

"Seems to know his business. Explains why he's so cautious, though, after his predecessor made such a big mistake. I can't believe they never caught the guy, in a town this small."

"Something happened, and they just stopped investigating. You know who'd know? Scooter. He's an Original Duck. He was in high school when it happened. He went away to college afterward, but he came back maybe a year or two ago. He would know, being the librarian. I'm surprised *you* didn't know this, though."

"Why would I know?"

Carinna looked uncomfortable. "Well, you know, with your mom and all."

"My mom? What about her?"

"Nothing. Just wondering."

"Tell me!"

"I don't really know anything. But you should ask Scooter. He was directly involved."

"In what?" I nearly shouted.

"Hey. I don't know, okay. Sorry I brought it up." She started to walk faster, and with her greater height and long legs I couldn't really keep up. I let her go.

I walked along slowly, hoping she'd double back, but she didn't.

In the space of six hours I'd managed to squabble with the only woman I knew in town and the handsomest, strangest librarian I'd ever met.

★ ★ ★

I guess that's what apologies are for. I was going to have to undo the mess I'd made.

But the more I thought about it, the more convinced I became that I wasn't in the wrong. For all the "no crime in Simpato" blather, people were hiding some pretty important stuff. Some of it pertained to my parents, and I was going to find out what.

Meanwhile, though, I had another vital task. I needed to get over to the storage unit before they closed at five. I wanted to look in that heavy box.

I threw the couple of sprung-out lawn chairs that belonged to my folks in the back of my car. No sense in wasting the trip. The Prius was muttering under its breath again. Something about the storage company didn't agree with my little red car, and as we approached the turn-in for the facility a number of warning lights flashed on the dashboard: *washer fluid, tire pressure, low battery?* Since these cars never break, I couldn't imagine how everything could go wrong at once. The ABS break light came on as I slowed to a stop at the entrance, and the car bucked back and forth before coming to a rest. Then all the warning lights went off and the car went silent.

Of course, these cars went silent anyway, I reminded myself as I pushed the ignition button off. When I first had the car, I left the engine on several times when I went into the grocery store, not realizing that the silence was just, well, silence.

I got out and went down the ramp to my unit, key in one hand, dragging the lawn chairs with the other. The office was dark; I guess Mrs. Cochrane had a lunch break at some point. I took out the key and fit it into the lock I'd bought from Mrs. Cochrane's little cash side-business. It stuck. I took it out and tried again. This time it slid in smoothly.

Then all went dark.

The light in the hall had gone out. "Damn!" I swore. I heard shuffling steps. "Mrs. Cochrane?" I said.

"Not quite," said a man's voice. "It's okay. I'll go switch it back on; it must have timed out."

I tried to place the voice but couldn't.

"Thanks," I called out.

And then something came over my head. "What the—" Something thick came across my mouth, and a strong arm wrapped around my throat. I struggled, kicking back against my assailant.

He cursed when my foot connected, but instead of loosening his grip like the self-defense classes said he would, he lifted me off my feet and threw me to the ground. I reached up to tear off whatever covered my face, but he was too quick. He wrapped something that felt like an electrical cord around my arms, pinning them to my sides. He turned me face-down on the cement floor and pressed me into the ground with his knee.

I stopped struggling.

"Better," he said. Another cord bound my ankles, and I thought of the real estate agent hogtied and drowned. I went limp and concentrated on staying alive and trying to place the voice. It wasn't Scooter's high whisper or the police chief's warm baritone. What other men's voices in town did I know? Officer Aureliano, Sergio, August. That was it, and this didn't sound like any of them. And yet, I thought I knew the voice.

At least he wasn't kneeling on me now, and I could somewhat breathe. The binding around my mouth was on the outside of whatever was over my head, so while I couldn't really talk and certainly not scream, I could breathe if I stayed calm.

I lay still and heard the door to my unit open. I heard rummaging around and then more swearing. There wasn't much in there, just the three boxes, and now my lawn furniture was on the floor in the hall. I hadn't bought a light-bulb, so he had to use his phone or a flashlight or something. But he wasn't finding whatever he was looking for.

Was it serendipity that he wanted to get into my unit and I happened to be there? No one knew I was coming over here. Had he been planning to break into it when I happened along?

A few more obscenities and then I sensed him standing over me. He grabbed my ankles. I struggled to kick him as he dragged me, my head bumping painfully on the ground, and I felt myself go over the small metal threshold of the storage unit. He was pulling me inside.

"Time to get some duck action!"

When he let go, I realized dragging me had moved the cord around my arms. I could free them with a little more work. I lay still, knowing I would need time to work the cord without his seeing if I was going to defend myself. I heard his breathing change and felt myself grow sick with dread.

He kicked the point of his shoe into my ribs, rolling me over onto my back. I tried to scream. "That's a girl," he said, then grabbed my ankles again. *No!*

I bucked against his hands and he cursed again. But he was trying to do something, and he pulled on my hands, making the cord slip further up my arms, nearly toward my shoulders. I started to fight him in earnest.

"Shit!" he said, pulling one of my hands toward my feet.

The other hand was now free. I made a fist and swung at where his face had to be.

I connected with wool.

He floundered, trying to grab my free hand while holding the other one. He was trying, I realized, to tie my hands to my feet.

Hogtied. Like the real estate agent who was murdered.

Suddenly I heard the door slam shut. "Hey!" he said. Even with whatever he'd put over my head, I could tell that we were now in total darkness.

Then my car alarm went off.

He scrambled around, and I heard the door open.

Through the cloth on my face, I could see a bit of light. I heard the sharp voice of Mrs. Cochrane, "What on earth!"

In her best fourth-grade-teacher voice she shouted "What do you think you're doing? Get out!" and I heard steps running down the hall. I went limp with relief.

"Oh, my dear. Let me get that off you," she said, pulling the cloth from my face. "Oh my god."

I watched as she dialed 911. Then she pulled the cord from my arms, and helped me sit up. "Looks like I was just in time," she said.

My eyes and nose were running, so I guess I was crying. I was also in shock.

"Who was it?" I asked.

"I don't know," she answered. "He was wearing a balaclava, and I didn't recognize his body. But his voice seemed familiar."

Painstakingly, she lowered herself to the floor and put an arm around me. "There, there," she crooned. "You're okay now."

We heard the sirens, and soon Luke Aureliano stood over me. "I'm calling the chief," he said. Then for the second time that day, Devon had a few questions for me.

* * *

I'd never ridden in the back of a police car before. The seats were hard plastic. "Easy to wipe clean," Devon Plata said. "I'd let you ride up front but I can't. It's seriously against protocol." There were seat belts, but they were stiff and had metal running through the cloth so they couldn't be cut. There was bulletproof glass between the back and the front seats. And a very nasty smell of old vomit.

"Mostly, we get drunks back there, on DUI arrests."

I used the ladies' room in the station before we went into the interview room. No cozy chat in Devon's office this time. I looked at my face, dirty and streaked with tears. I had a bruise forming above my eyebrow, and my lip was slightly swollen.

He'd offered a ride to the local hospital, but I'd declined. I was shaken, most definitely, but not injured. Though that rib was starting to ache.

Sergio brought me a big glass of water and another cup of coffee. He was going to get to sit in again, since Luke Aureliano had to deal with the "location issues."

"Such as prints, interviewing Mrs. Cochrane," Devon said. With my permission, he was also going to search my boxes.

"Is it just the three of you, then?" I asked. "The whole police department?"

Devon shook his head. "We have four guys on the two night shifts and a traffic enforcer. You've seen her, I'm sure. She tickets people who park overtime and drivers who go into the crosswalk while some old lady is only a quarter of the way across. And we have a clerk who comes in twice a week to type and file. But yeah, three during the day, and a weekend relief from the county sheriff when we end up with too much overtime."

More than I wanted to know.

"Plus," he said, "we've called in the sheriff's office for this one. It's really more than we can handle, with Ms. Noyes, Mr. Solis, and you."

They were Ms. and Mr. now. "You didn't find the mayor, did you?" As in, *dead*.

"No, but it doesn't look good. Now, let's go through this slowly."

I told him each step. "Did you tell anyone that you were going to the storage unit?" I shook my head *no*. "Answer out loud, please." It was a formal interview; it was being recorded.

When I reached the part where I was tied up on the ground, I hesitated. Did I tell him I knew about the real estate agent's murder?

Devon turned to Sergio, indicated without speaking that he wanted the recorder off. Sergio turned it off. "Do you want me to call in our traffic enforcer?"

"What? Why?" I was confused.

"I need to ask some other questions, and I thought you might want a policewoman here, even if she's only a cadet."

"That's really thoughtful," I said, "but he didn't . . ."

Devon nodded. "I know he didn't. Sergio, call Tilly." Sergio leapt up from his chair and was gone before the chief could change his mind.

Devon turned to me. "Look, Sal. I know there's *no crime in Simpato*, but this guy was up to something really not good. Whether it was planned or just bad luck again, you were there. I need to ask you some very intimate questions. We may know who he is, if it's what I think. So let's wait for Tilly to join us. I think you, and definitely I, will feel more comfortable."

I felt sicker than I did in the storage unit. My sense had been right.

"But can I ask a question?" I was a lot more humble now.

"Of course. I may not be able to answer it, though."

I took a deep breath. "I heard about the real estate agent that was murdered ten years ago."

"Nine."

"Okay, but he was found," I gulped, "hogtied and drowned in the Valley River. I'm wondering . . . I'm pretty sure . . . was that what he was going to do? It was like he was trying to tie me up like that."

Devon chewed his lip a moment. "I don't know, Sal. That was a long time ago. And we've had a couple of incidents far more recently—"

A timid knock brought in a muscular-looking young woman with her hair back in a tight bun. I was struck by the fact that she was probably the first Black woman I'd seen in Simpato. How strange. "Chief?"

"Tilly, this is Salvia DeVine. She's a new resident of Simpato, and she was attacked at the storage facility. Attempted."

I started to interrupt but thought better of it.

"Ms. DeVine," so in the presence of this young cadet he leapt into the twenty-first century and used Ms., "this is Tilda Green; she's a police cadet, waiting for her final exams in June. If all goes well, and we have every expectation that it will, she'll be joining our force here in Simpato. Meanwhile, don't park for more than three hours downtown." He smiled. She didn't.

"Have a seat, put the recorder on, state your name, and we'll keep going. Sergio was assisting, but the complaining witness wanted a female officer, and we thought it best."

Again, I started to say something. But let Devon handle his personnel as he saw fit.

He turned back to me. "Ms. DeVine, I'm going to ask some questions starting with the moment you were attacked. Please be as detailed as you can be. Even if it's hard." I nodded.

He took me through the whole thing again. "When the assailant pulled you into the locker, did he say anything?"

I thought back, chills running down my arms. Both were looking hard at me. He had said something. About ducks. "Something about ducks. Duck action."

Both of them exhaled at once.

"And when he kicked me and I tried to scream, he said, *that's a girl.*"

"And then he grabbed your ankles and lifted them?" Devon asked. I nodded. "Answer out loud."

"Yes. But he was trying to tie my hands to them, and that worked the cord off my other arm, and I slugged him in the face."

Tilly smiled. "What did he feel like?" she asked. "You were still blinded, right?"

"Yeah," I said. "It felt like wool."

She looked over at Devon. "It's the same guy, I'm sure of it."

"But he tried to go through my boxes first!" I exclaimed.

Devon nodded. "There's a tie-in here. I don't know what yet, but there is. Let's see what Luke comes up with, if anything. They're dusting for prints and looking in the boxes. Who knows. Thank you, Tilly. We're good now."

"Wait, Chief. Ms. DeVine, did the attacker do anything else? Try to pull your jeans down or put his hands up your shirt?"

"No, thank god."

"Thank god is right."

She got up to leave. "You live in the old Keeper's house now, right?"

"I'm her daughter."

She looked at Devon, but he had schooled his face into expressionlessness. She shrugged.

"Thanks, Tilly," he said again. She gave me a look, and her eyebrow moved just the tiniest bit. I nodded slightly. We'd talk later.

As soon as the door shut, Devon sat back in his chair. "I'm going to ask you a big favor. Two big favors, actually."

I waited.

He hesitated. "Easy one first: can you not talk to anyone, especially not to Carinna, or really anyone, about what happened? And not the *Quack*. Just for a few days?" I nodded. "Okay. And second, tomorrow is Tuesday. Some rumors are going around that you're going to have some Keeper's Hours tomorrow. Is that true?"

"No, not really. I mean, some people have pestered me about that, but frankly, I have no idea at all about what's entailed. But someone on Facebook suggested I be available on Tuesday—"

"Who?" he nearly shouted.

"I don't know. I can look at my phone, but it's all funny names, not regular ones. Business names with Duck in them."

"The WAD page?" I nodded. "Okay. I'll look."

"And I didn't say no. So, since you don't want me to, I just won't."

"No. It's the other way around. I want you to do it. Tomorrow. Say from four to six."

"But I have no idea what's involved!"

"As far as I know—I mean, I never talked to your mother in that role—you just sit out on your back deck, and people come and tell you their secrets. Like confession, you know."

"I'm Jewish, not Catholic. We only have confession once a year, and it's between you and God."

He smiled. "Probably more honest that way. But this is more like Catholic confession, in that it's in person, but it isn't necessarily one's sins. And you don't hand out penance, Hail Marys or what have you. Or absolution. Just a chance to get stuff off their chests, or their conscience. And the Keeper never tells. Usually."

"Wait. Usually?"

He swallowed. "If you get any information about any of this, anything at all, I want you to tell me."

"So, betray their trust?"

He was quiet for a moment. "If we're dealing with a murderer or a rapist, yes. The rest, no. From what I know, your mother would have done it."

"From what I knew of my mother, she wouldn't."

Devon looked me in the eye. *She would, and she did,* his face said. Then he looked away. "Up to you."

"Can I think about it?"

He nodded. "But don't think too long. Meanwhile, we'll have an officer drive by your house every hour or so, just to keep an eye on things."

For a place with no crime . . .

And then Aureliano entered without knocking. "Chief, I need to see you now."

Devon glanced at me. "Ok, Sal, let me know as soon as you decide. Go on home, you could probably use a rest."

"Uh, no, Chief. I think she should stay." Devon's eyebrows went up. "And besides, she'll need a ride to the storage place to get her car."

My Prius, whose alarm may have saved my life.

"Fine. Wait here, if you don't mind," Devon said to me. "Come on, Luke," he said, walking out, "what's this about?" Aureliano closed the door with a click.

★ ★ ★

I wasn't left alone long. The door opened again, and Tilly poked her head around. "Mind if I come in?" she asked.

"I've never had a cop ask if she could come in to her own interview room," I said. "Pull up a chair."

"I brought you some coffee. They have really good coffee here."

I nodded. "I've had about six cups already, but thanks. I'll take it."

She sat down across from me and took a sip of her own cup. I noticed that her hands and wrists were slender, as was her neck. It was likely the amount of equipment she had to wear that made her so stocky-looking.

"Does all that stuff they make you wear get tiring?" I asked.

"Heck yeah. I had no idea, back in the day, I thought all cops were fat. This vest alone," she opened her collar to show me, "weighs about five pounds. The ones the guys wear weigh about eight because they're bigger. It's like carrying a baby, and still having to run and jump and all."

She must be about twenty-two, I thought. Her face looked

about twelve. She smiled. "I bet you're thinking there aren't a lot of Black folks here in Simpato."

"I thought that earlier. You may be the first I've seen. Kind of like Jewish people. Not a lot of us, either, but you can't tell."

She nodded. "There's, like, ten families in Simpato. Black families. Not Black-Latino, you know."

"You grow up here?"

She nodded. "I'm an OD. Original Duck. Went to Simpato High, known as No-Duck High to the parents, and you can guess what the kids called it." I laughed. "So, mind if we talk a bit, sort of unofficially?"

"What exactly does that mean, *sort of unofficially*?"

She shrugged. "The chief knows I'm talking to you. But I'm not recording anything, not taking notes. I may or may not tell him what we talk about, but if it's important, I will."

"Sounds official enough to me. But go ahead. What's on your mind?"

"No one asks me that anymore! But that's exactly it. You know how everyone says there's no crime in Simpato?" I nodded. "But that's not true. There isn't a lot, you can leave something on your porch and no one's going to steal it, that kind of thing, but there is something going on right now that is really not good." She took a deep breath.

"About a week ago, my neighbor's little sister, no more than fourteen, was walking home from an after-school ceramics club meeting. She was on the road out near the lake. A couple of men were walking toward her, coming off the lake path. She knew one, the librarian, because he's so incredibly hot, and the other was the mayor. They were arguing about something. The librarian has that funny voice, and he was trying to yell at Mayor Solis. Because he has that funny voice, my neighbor, Leticia, started laughing. You know how fourteen-year-olds are.

"So they stopped, and she said hi to them and kept walking.

The next day, she was out in the morning on her run, she's on the track team and runs all year, every morning at seven she goes around the lake, rain or shine, super-disciplined.

"Someone grabbed her. Pulled her to the ground and covered her face with a towel. Then he tried to pull her shorts down. But she's a strong little thing, and wiry, and she hit and scratched and screamed and got away. She heard him try to catch her, but she's a real fast runner. She made it home and called me."

I was breathing hard, and so was Tilly. This was definitely bad.

"The one thing the bastard said was, *Gonna get some duck action,* and *be a good girl,* same stuff he said to you. The thing is, that's what the guys at the high school used to call getting laid: getting some duck action. So it's someone local. And no one has reported actually getting raped. Just trying. Which is why the chief wanted me to sit in. Besides being a female officer and all. In case the guy did more to you, and you didn't want to tell him."

After a while, during which I quelled my impulse to pat Tilly's hand to comfort her, I said, "So do you, and the police in general, think that this attack was related to seeing the mayor and Scooter that day?"

She shrugged. "We don't know. And to attack you, even though you're pretty small, that's just crazy. But the only thing is you're involved somehow in this thing with the mayor and Mrs. Noyes, and the development and all. So I wanted to know, did he do anything more to you?"

I exhaled. "No. I told the chief everything. But it's wonderful that Simpato has you. And that the protocol is to put a woman on a rape accusation, to help the victim come forward. I think you will be an incredible asset to the department. It sounds like this guy, this rapist or would-be rapist, is pretty indiscriminate: a fourteen-year-old, a forty-five-year-old . . ."

"Yeah, he doesn't seem to have a *type.* But this is a very serious crime, and we really don't have this kind of thing here. We have to catch this guy. Did anyone take any samples from your hands or anything? Under your nails?"

I shook my head. "I only got one swing on him, and I hit wool. And Mrs. Cochrane is the one who came to my rescue—"

"I had her for fourth grade!"

"Seems like everyone did. She didn't recognize him either."

"She works at the storage facility now, that's right. I wonder what the guy was doing there? And did he follow you over or was it luck—I mean, bad luck—he was lurking there?"

"It sounded like he opened my storage boxes, too. Like he was looking for something and didn't find it."

She looked at me, tipping her head a bit to the side, like she was deciding whether to tell me something or not. What she said instead was, "You gonna be the Keeper? Like the chief asked?"

"How did you know that?"

"We talked about it ahead. I think it's the only way we can solve this. This and the killing of Mrs. Noyes."

The door opened, and Chief Plata, Devon, came in.

"Please stay seated, Mrs. DeVine."

Mrs. DeVine. Oh dear.

CHAPTER EIGHT

Chief Plata, at this moment *not Devon*, pulled up a chair, as did Officer Luke Aureliano. Cadet Officer Tilda Green was invited to remain. Aureliano had the recorder. "Ms. DeVine," Plata started, "did you put everything in your boxes yourself before taking them to storage, or did anyone help you?"

"I did it myself. The only help I had was from August, who came by and helped move them, first onto my back deck, and later out of the rain, and then put them in his truck and helped me take them to storage."

I answered clearly. I had a feeling I knew where this was going.

"August Sanjusto?"

"I don't know his last name."

"There were three boxes in your storage unit; one was open. There were only a couple of older lawn chairs and some curtains there as well. Did you move the lawn chairs in, and the curtains, at the same time?"

I stopped to think. "No. Yes. The lawn chairs I threw in my car at the last moment just before I went over this time; they were my folks' chairs, and they were in lousy condition. I was going to throw them out, but this way I could donate them or something. The curtains . . . wait, the curtains were in the box."

"So what did you take over in your car?"

I tried to picture the whole thing, but I hadn't been suspicious, so I hadn't made myself notice anything. "I took one of the boxes. August helped me get it into my car. I thought all three would fit—spatial relations aren't my thing—but they are August's, and he knew they wouldn't."

"So you took one of the boxes yourself." I nodded. "Out loud."

"Yes. So, what was in the box?" I asked.

"You tell us."

"I did the first day. Books, some items that wouldn't fit in the house, my parents' old curtains. More books."

Plata gestured to Aureliano. "Did you put anything that wasn't from your house in the boxes?" Aureliano asked.

"No. What did you find?"

Aureliano sighed, and suddenly looked very young. "One box had been opened, and the curtains you mentioned were on the floor. So were the two pieces of lawn furniture. Mrs. Cochrane said she pushed them in and closed your unit's door. She gave me the key, which was still in the lock. The other two boxes were closed, like with flaps tucked. Not sealed. And in one, under a bunch of law books, was a rock."

"A rock?"

"A rock. How did that get in your box?"

"I have no idea. Can I see it?"

"You don't want to."

I was silent. Why wouldn't I . . . oh.

I felt myself getting nauseous. Tilly got up and brought me a glass of water. "Steady there," she said.

I sipped. "Thanks." When the room stopped spinning, I looked over at Plata. "I have no idea. Was it the rock that . . . that killed," I whispered the word, "Georgiana Noyes?"

"Looks that way. I won't go into detail, but it would appear so. They will have to do some testing at the county lab, hopefully quickly. I really wish you'd seen the guy who attacked you. Or scratched him hard enough to get some DNA under your nails or something."

I did too. But I didn't.

"Well, we know he's tall and thin, from Mrs. Cochrane."

"And he's a white guy," Tilly said. "Leticia saw his hands and his neck. And you did get something from her nails. But she keeps them so short, because she does ceramics."

"Yeah, the lab said there was a lot of clay," Aureliano added.

Everyone was quiet. "I think you're free to go," Chief Plata said and leaned forward, *Devon* once again. "I'll stop by later, make sure you're okay."

"Thanks," I said. I stood up shakily. "Can I get a ride back to the storage facility? Or should I call a Lyft?"

"I'll drive you," Tilly said. "It's four, and I'm off now." She glanced at Plata, who nodded. "It's on my way."

"Oh, and Mrs. DeVine?" Aureliano said. "Mrs. Cochrane said she'd give you an extra day to get your insurance, otherwise you'd be cancelled at the end of the day."

★ ★ ★

At 8:05 that evening, long after it was dark, the front doorbell rang. I jumped. I'd not heard it before, since in my brief time here people had either knocked, like Sister Sorghum, or just shown up on my back deck. Or honked the hell out of their horn. I looked through the peephole. It was Chief Devon Plata.

I let him in.

"Long day. I saw you at ten this morning, and you got off at eight?"

"Yep. It's my twelve day. We're short-staffed. Even with Tilly coming on in July." He had added a navy-blue sweater over his checked blue-and-white collared shirt, and it brought out his eyes in bright relief. But he looked tired, and adding this stop to check on me was yet another burden in an over-burdened life.

"You can see I'm okay, physically at least," I said. "I'm happy to have you sit down and relax a bit if you wish, but don't feel obligated."

He looked at me like he was trying to decide. "It's an off-duty call, my choice," he said finally. "I'm concerned about the situation we've got, and you're right smack in the center of it."

I didn't mind. "What can I get you? I have wine, sparkling water, and I can make coffee or tea."

"Wine would be nice. What have you got?" He looked over the selection. "This white is really nice; it's unusual for here. Not a lot of Chenin Blanc grown in the Valley."

"You're a connoisseur?"

"We all kind of get to be. In Oregon, we grow a lot of white varieties, because it's cooler. Down here, with the blazing hot summers, it takes a special microclimate to grow these."

I guess he *was* a bit of a connoisseur. I poured him a glass, and poured a half for myself. It hits me too hard to allow a full glass with a stranger. Especially a cop. "Your wife won't mind your stopping by?" I said, handing him his glass.

"Artfully asked," he smiled as he made himself comfortable in the stuffed chair. "Divorced for ten years, a bit more. How about you?"

"Divorce finalized a month ago this coming Friday. Since we're talking personal, any kids?"

He nodded. "Two. A boy, Alexander, we call him Alex, fin-ishing his first year at Oregon State, Ashland. He's a theater guy. And a daughter, Rachel, graduated U of O, getting a teaching cre-dential in English. Bunch of wordsmiths in my family. How about you?" he asked, looking around for any sign of kids.

"Nope. I've got a cat, but my ex seems to think he has cus-tody. My sister, Dahlia, takes care of the procreation part of family. She lives in Maui and reads Tarot cards for a living. Three boys."

"Aunts are very important—" He stopped suddenly. "Where did you get those glasses?"

I followed his look. "Those? Pretty, aren't they? They were left on my doorstep the morning after . . . no on Saturday morning. All this terrible excitement has mixed up my days for me."

"Do you know who left them?"

"No, why? They're pretty, but I don't know who left them. I guess they're a welcome-to- Simpato present. The card or whatever must have blown off in the rain we had."

He shook his head. "They're from the monastery. Very special glasses, they have. Have you had anything out of them yet?"

That sounded dangerous. "No, I just put them there after I opened them. I didn't even wash them yet, which I would have done anyway before I drank out of them. Why?"

He sighed heavily. "I promise I'll tell you later, but for now can I take the glasses?"

I was flummoxed. As a lawyer, I was inclined not to let him take anything without a warrant. As a human, I was willing to do whatever was needed to solve this—what? Murder? The disappearance of the mayor? The attack on Tilly's little neighbor? The attack on me? All of it.

I stood up, and got some paper towels from the kitchen. I started wrapping them when he said, "No. Stop. Let me take them. Don't add anything."

I put the glass down. "I have the paper that they came in, and the box too, here in my recycling bin, if you think it will help. It was some pages from the *Quack*—"

He stood up so fast he spilled some wine on the floor. "Yes. Don't touch anything about them. Let me—oh, sorry." He looked down at the wine on the floor and on his pant leg.

"No problem. I'll just put these paper towels to good use."

I handed the towels to him and he mopped up, first his pants then the floor. "Composting?" I showed him the green container. Then he pulled a pair of examination gloves out of his pocket.

"Travel with those?" I asked.

He nodded, putting them on. "Never know when you're going to need them."

What a weird life.

I handed him the pages of the *Quack* and the box. He glanced at the paper. "Great."

"Really great or *oh great*?"

"Really great. Good distinction."

"You're not the only wordsmith," I said. "What's great about it?"

"Either the choice is coincidental or deliberate, but it's got the articles about the mayor right there, and the newspaper isn't smudged, if you know what I mean, so there may be prints. Besides yours. And, we will need to take your fingerprints tomorrow. I should have had Sergio do it the first day. Tomorrow, okay? I'll let them know, since I'm off."

"Off with a murderer and possibly a rapist loose?"

He smiled a bit. "There are others. Tomorrow we have someone from the county Sheriff's office in, so you'll be in good hands."

"You mentioned that you called in the Sheriff?"

"That's how we work up here. We do have our own station, not all small towns do, but there are eight of us all told, soon to be nine. Think about it. We need at least two, if not three officers on duty all the time. With eight-hour shifts we lose coverage for more than sixteen hours a week if we just have two on. Four of us, we rotate every month, take one twelve-hour day the day before we're off. That limits overtime. But we also need a third, at least three or four shifts a week. And Saturday night. And in the summer, when there are more tourists.

"So we get guys from the Sheriff's office who want a little overtime, since their schedules aren't as spread out. And like I told you, we have two clerks, which helps a lot with paperwork, but they're part-timers. But you don't want to hear about my personnel problems."

I was watching him as he spoke, and as he gently wrapped the glasses and box. It was as if there were two people: the careful policeman taking a piece of evidence—though evidence of what I had no clue—and the head of Human Resources. I mentioned it.

"That's what being the chief is. You nailed it."

★ ★ ★

The glasses carefully put to bed, we sat and enjoyed the bottle of wine. I put out some cheese and crackers, the creamy Cambozola working well with the Chenin Blanc, and talked about everything but the situation at hand.

"I met Jenny in college. I was a senior and she was a sophomore, and I was getting ready to apply to law schools when she got pregnant. We got married at Christmastime, and I enrolled in criminal-justice classes for the last semester. I was working as a security guard part-time, and her folks helped out, and we didn't question what we had to do. We're both Catholics, and we were in love, and she hated school anyway. She wanted to teach Pilates. After Rachel was born, I started at the police academy, and Alex was born when I was a new officer.

"Jenny worked at a local spa, and things were pretty good; we were always short on cash but otherwise we were pretty happy. But more and more I was never home, and she had the little ones, and I would get all wrapped up in some of the uglier crimes. Meth was taking over—"

He stopped.

I waited.

"And one night I found myself in a pretty tough spot with a gang. I got the young girl out, took her to the hospital, but it was bad. And when I came back to the station, the chief sent me home. I was shaking so hard I could barely drive. It was about three in the morning, I walked into my house, and Jenny was in bed with another man."

Wow.

"I was so tired I slept on the couch, and when I woke up the next morning, Alex, my boy, said, 'Hey dad! You're home! Does that mean you'll take me to school today instead of Steve?' Well, you can imagine. We filed for divorce, and the knife in my heart was Alex taking it in stride that *Steve* would be taking him to school every morning from then on. Uh, forgot to ask you, what kind of law do you do?"

I felt myself blush. Not the time for the whole suspension story, definitely. "Estates. Wills. Not divorces," I added with a smile. "Hell of a story, Devon. So you moved here?"

"A bit later. A lot of counseling later. Rachel was fourteen and didn't speak to me for almost a year. Even though it was her mother who'd been unfaithful. She saw it as all my fault, and after enough counseling sessions I understood why."

"You good with the kids now?"

He nodded. "As good as any dad can be. Alex used to come for the summer. Rache didn't. But she'd spend a weekend now and then. She's still edgy with me."

I poured the last of the wine into our glasses. "We killed the bottle," I said. "You going to be okay to drive?"

It wouldn't do to have the police chief stopped for a DUI. He nodded.

"Besides, you need to tell me about the glasses," I said. "Let's switch to coffee and I'll make some sandwiches."

★ ★ ★

I rinsed the sandwich plates in the sink while Devon rummaged for coffee cups. "The glasses?" I reminded him.

"Those pretty glasses are part of a collection from the monastery. Either one of the nuns dropped them off as a housewarming present—"

"I got two cookies from Sister Sorghum for a housewarming."

"Did you eat them?"

"Tossed them. Not my drug of choice."

"Have you taken the trash out yet?"

We retrieved the cookies, and he put them by the door with the glasses. "There's a bite taken out of one," he said.

"Spat it out. They taste horrible. What's this all about?" I asked. "You don't think the nuns killed Georgiana Noyes, do you? I don't think she gossiped about them!"

"I don't know how much I should tell you, but here goes. Georgiana Noyes is, was, a city council member. She was in favor of the development and opposed to the mayor. The mayor was against, well, *this* development."

"There are two, aren't there?"

He nodded. "Sort of. Two, in the sense that about a dozen years ago, before my time, there was a big dispute about developing a parcel that's currently planted to vineyards, south of town. It turned out that it was owned in part by Georgiana, not openly but she was part of some LLC, this all before my time and, I don't really understand what an LLC is anyway—" he held up his hand to stop me as I leaned forward, ready to explain how limited liability companies worked.

"But the head guy of that LLC was a local real estate agent. They were gung-ho about developing it, and they were just about to break ground when Sebastian Solis led a really bruising and public campaign against the development, making the agent look like a slimy worm. Then the agent wound up dead."

"Hogtied and drowned in the Valley River, right?"

"You know this already? From your mom?"

"My mother? What does she have to do with it?"

"Well, she was the Keeper, right? So I guess she knew, and I figured she told you at some point."

"Nope. Never breathed a word. I really want to know more about this Keeper business, especially if you think I'm going to do it starting, what, tomorrow?" I looked at my watch. "Today."

"It's that late? I really need to get to bed. Look, I'll tell you more tomorrow, okay. I'll stop by, off-duty, sometime tomorrow, I'll text you first, if that works for you." He stood, stretched. Good-looking man, I thought.

"Sure, that would be nice."

"Don't forget though. Go get your prints taken. Sergio's on tomorrow. He can do it."

"Always on duty, eh, Chief?" I said with a smile. The look he gave me broke my heart.

"Sorry." It must have been a painful echo.

CHAPTER NINE

My prints duly recorded, I walked a few blocks toward the west end of town. I hadn't done a lot of exploring on this side. The street was filled with early tourists, and the weather was bright and just warm around the edges, the way a Spring day can be. Little shops with pastel-colored dresses and parasols in the windows promised a brilliant summer, and a florist had put buckets filled with flowers along the sidewalk in front of her store. Beyond the florist, the door was open to a coffee shop, and the smell of fresh donuts made my mouth water.

I had just a touch of a headache from last night's wine. I went in and ordered a coffee and a French cruller, taking them to a table on the sidewalk. Parklets for outdoor dining had been set up during the pandemic, and everyone liked them so much they stayed. Someone always had a gripe about their taking up three or four parking spaces but other than that, it gave a gay, Parisian, or at least vacation feel to everyday snacks.

Across the street was the library. I was surprised at how big the building was. It took up nearly a quarter of the block and looked like an old bank. I watched as a mother took her pre-schooler in, and then another, and then one with two kids, just beyond toddlers, both with long black braids down their backs. Must be children's story hour.

I reviewed my evening with Chief Plata. I would definitely

have to call him Devon after that exchange of confidences. Or more accurately, his confidences. The more I thought about that the more unlikely it seemed that it would have played out that way. He's the police chief, why would he be spilling his guts to me, a stranger? I was sure it wasn't strategic. I supposed that being the chief of police in a very small town could be very lonely. Or very, very social.

It would be very telling how he reacted to me when he stopped by later today, if he did. Would he be gruff to cover embarrassment? Or overly formal?

Across the street a banner flapped in the breeze. I stood and peered at it. "Duck into Reading!"

"Looking for me?" I jumped as the high, whispery voice of the librarian whistled in my ear.

Scooter was standing slightly behind me, a paper coffee cup in one hand and the biggest elephant-ear pastry I'd ever seen in the other.

I took a step away, clearing some personal space. "Not exactly, but I'm not sorry to have run into you," I answered. "Join me?" I sat back down.

"I need to go make sure the preschool reading program is going okay, then I'll come back. Mind if I set my snack down on your table? You know, sort of bail for my return."

I shrugged. "Sure. If I eat the elephant ear, does that mean you're released from returning?" He smiled and loped across the street, long legs taking the lanes in a few steps.

"Don't be fooled by his good looks," Carinna appeared next to the empty chair. It looked like this cafe was the Grand Central Station of Simpato. "Sit here long enough and you'll meet everyone in town."

"Actually," I said. This was awkward. "He's coming back. This is his food." And this is his chair. I made a decision. "Come by later? Are you free?"

Carinna looked down at me, clearly weighing something.

"Sure," she said finally. "I'll be around after, say, two. And," she paused, "I want to apologize for storming off yesterday."

"Was it only yesterday?" I asked. My god, so much had happened. "No worries. But we need to talk about something, so please do come over. Two would be great."

"I'll be at the monastery until then," she said. "You've got my cell if something changes."

I saw Scooter stop, just as he put one foot out into the road. He had seen Carinna. She looked up. "Got to go. Like I said, don't be taken in."

Scooter crossed much more slowly this time. "The White Lady spreading her good cheer?" he said. He pulled out his chair without waiting for an answer.

"All well with the preschoolers?"

"Huh? Oh, yeah. Ysenia has them well in hand." He bit into the pastry, flakes falling everywhere. He wiped his mouth with the back of his hand. I handed him a napkin. "Thanks, mom," he said.

True. He was what, twenty-eight? Twenty-nine? And I was forty-five. So yeah, *mom*. If I'd been a teen-aged mother, that is. But still.

"I want to have a serious talk with you," he said once most of the elephant ear was gone. "But not here. Let's take a walk."

I frowned. "Why not here? Or, do you have a little office in the library?"

"Not here because I want some privacy. Not the library because little ducklings have big bills."

I had to smile at that one. "Fine." I stood up. He stuffed the last of the pastry in his mouth and gulped the last of his coffee. Ah, youth. "Where to?"

"No-Duck Lake is a nice stroll," he said.

"That's at least eight blocks, or nine, from here," I said.

"Uh uh," he shook his head. "By Main Street it is, but it's just, like, three-and-a-half via Peaches."

I recalled making that same discovery coming down from Cragstown. "So Central Avenue kind of curves?" He nodded. "And Peaches goes up to the road to Cragstown?" He stopped, looked down at me. After a moment, another nod. After all, geography was geography. I took out my phone and looked at the map. Sure enough, Central circled nearly around to where Carinna and I had walked. I pressed the side buttons for a screen shot.

"Still learning my way around," I smiled.

And we were there. At the end of Simpato Lake, from the other side.

"Our own Duckless Pond," Scooter said.

It was beautiful. The water was shimmering, and reeds poked up, green and fresh, through the water all along the edge. The sun, now high in the sky, reflected brightly in my eyes. I shielded them with one hand and looked out at the mountain rising sharply above the vineyards. I took another photo.

"This way," Scooter said, leading me toward the vineyards. "There's an amazing view from over here."

I found Devon's cell in contacts, put it into my text, and sent him a copy of my photo. "Walking with Scooter," I added quickly, then pushed send. The little circle went around. I put the phone away. It would send when it could.

It dawned on me that Carinna was right about the cell reception. At least here. Why did Aureliano disagree so vehemently?

"What did you want to talk about?" I asked. I couldn't see anyone else on the trail, and it was just a bit uncomfortable walking with Scooter alone.

He sighed. "You gonna be the Keeper?"

"I wish to heck someone would tell me what that's all about!"

★ ★ ★

We stopped at the edge of the vineyard. It didn't look like the same place Carinna and I had walked, because the trail led to the left, to a different part of the mountain. Not far, but not the same.

"Look down," he said. I did. It was, indeed, lovely. "See that holding pond? The irrigation one is different from the lake; you can see the steep edges angling down to the water, as opposed to the gentle sides of the lake." I nodded. "But the edges of the lake get deep real quick," he said. I felt a shiver start in my stomach.

"When I was eighteen, I'm a bit old for my class, learning issues, so I was just starting my senior year, we used to come up here to drink and smoke weed, like everyone else. Me, and August, and even Sergio sometimes, though he was a lot younger and his mom was strict as hell. And a guy named Carl. Carl Montefusco. Amazing athlete, he was on the football team, and the soccer team—which is a hell of a lot bigger deal here—and we were both on the baseball team, though he wasn't a track guy like me. He was probably the most popular guy in the school. Which meant he could get any girl he wanted, any kind of duck action he wanted, right?"

I nodded, though I wasn't sure that was always the case. *Duck action.* What a phrase. Where had I heard—at the storage facility. I froze.

"But Carl, well, he was just a little off. Not like August, I mean, August has always been a little, I don't know, slow, right? But there was something about Carl that we couldn't figure out. Because we were stupid kids, right?" Again he waited for me to nod.

"Well, Carl's dad was a real estate agent, big wheeler dealer, here in town, and there was something off about him too. We were scared of Mr. Montefusco, I can't remember his first name because he was Mister to us, not like some parents who didn't mind if you called them by their first names, except the Spanish ones, them you called Señor or Señora, but without a last name. Who knows why. Just the Duck way, I guess."

Scooter started walking again, away from the lake. He looked back at me. I followed.

"What about Carl's mom?" I said, to say something.

"She died when Carl was about four. His dad raised him. But that wouldn't have changed anything, kids are born that way. I read up on it."

"What way?"

He stopped. "Kind of mean, I guess. But funny-mean, unless you were the one he was being mean to. Then it wasn't that funny. You know what I'm saying?" Again, I nodded. "So to make a long story short, Carl's dad died too, and he went to live in LA with an aunt, even though he was almost eighteen, didn't get to graduate with the class or anything."

He walked on. "Slow down, Scott," I said. I stopped walking. I really didn't want to go any further. "What happened to Carl?"

"Come on, let's go down." He seemed to have changed his mind about telling me whatever was on his mind. He strode past me once again, ahead of me on the downslope.

"Poor Carl," I said. "First his mom, then his dad. What was it, a heart attack?" I tried to keep it light, making conversation, but I had just realized who Carl's dad must have been. I knew what had happened to him.

Scooter turned around. I almost ran into him. "Give me your phone."

"What? Why?"

His big hand went around my wrist. "Give it to me. I want to see your phone."

I tried to yank my hand away, but he was far, far stronger. His whispery voice could still convey his menace. He pulled my phone from my pocket. With an overhand a pro would have envied, he threw it. I heard the splash. I screamed.

"Stop!" he rasped. He put another huge hand over my mouth.

"Stop! I'm not going to hurt you. Stop!" He pulled me into him. A small part of my mind was telling me this was not the same person who'd attacked me in the storage facility. That he actually wasn't going to harm me.

"You took my phone," I said. "I can't believe you did that."

"I'm sorry," he whispered. "I didn't mean to scare you. I'll buy you a new one. Send me the bill. I'm sorry." He was shaking. I was shaking. What the hell? "I just don't want stuff recorded. And phones record stuff, even when you don't want them to. What you say, you know how you get ads for the same stuff right afterward? And where you've been? Right?"

"Right," I said quickly, and started down past the vineyard. How quickly could I get away from him? And how would I get in touch with the police?

"This happens to me," he said, walking behind me. I had to strain to hear him. "Too many concussions or something. I go wild. I just . . . I'm sorry."

"It's okay," I lied. I needed to get back to town. I checked my watch. Almost one. I would go straight to the police.

"But you're the Keeper now, so you can't tell anyone."

I wouldn't bet on that, but I knew enough to keep my mouth shut.

"You going to have hours this evening? That's what everyone's saying."

I was walking down the hill as fast as I could without running. Somehow, I knew that if I started to run he would be like an animal seeing prey. Something had already triggered Scooter, and there was no way on earth I could outrun him anyway.

"You gonna be the Keeper tonight?" he repeated.

I had to do it. Whatever it entailed, I knew I had to. But as Devon had requested, I was going to tell him if anything came up. "Maybe. If I do, it will be from five to seven tonight. Don't hog the time."

He laughed. "No, ma'am." It was like a switch had been pulled. He was back to being the town librarian. I needed to get away. We got to the corner where we could see Peaches. There were people walking, cars going by. I sped up.

Scooter came close and whispered, "Tonight I'll tell you what happened to Carl."

★ ★ ★

As soon as I got away from Scooter I reached for my phone—amazing how reflexive that was, like turning on the light switch when the power went out. I had time to walk over to the police station, but who would I tell? Chief Devon was off today. Luke Aureliano? Who said there was plenty of cell reception? Maybe he was right about the side where we'd been, but if the cell tower was there, it would have sent my text. Maybe my text was sent. But I wouldn't know.

And what would I tell him? That I had voluntarily taken a walk with Scooter, even though he made me nervous, up to the lake? And Scooter had told me about Carl Montefusco, whose father had been murdered ten years ago? And that I'd almost deliberately goaded him to tell me what happened to Mr. Montefusco, senior? Well, he took my phone and threw it in the lake, and that, at least, was worth reporting.

When I got to the police station, only Sergio was there. "Officer Aureliano is out in the field, and no one else is on today. Can I help you?"

"Wasn't there supposed to be someone from the sheriff's office on today too?" I asked.

Sergio didn't seem surprised that I knew. "Yeah, he called in sick. Luke called the chief, the chief said he would try to come in later, and we had coverage this morning from the night shift. One of the guys took a twelve to cover the morning until Luke got here. Is there something I can help you with?"

I thought about it for a second. He was one of the boys who used to hang out drinking and smoking above the lake when the other boys were seniors. He sometimes went to bars with August. It might be better not to tell him. "When did the chief say he'd come in?"

"Maybe eight tonight."

"Maybe you can help me. I'm supposed to be the new Keeper. Any idea how I go about it?"

He chuckled. "Nothing to it. My mom used to go all the time. Just put your chairs on your deck, and folks come by and talk to you. Because you'll never tell. *Mejor que el padre,* my mom used to say. Better than the priest. Because the Keeper didn't make you pray afterward. You'll be fine."

"Okay. I'm going to give it a try tonight from five to seven."

"Cool. I'll come by, okay? Make sure it's all going smooth." He puffed up a little with that. "Chief said to keep an eye on you, keep you safe. So that's going to be my plan."

"Thanks," I said. "Oh, one more thing. Where's the nearest phone store? I need to get a new one."

"What happened to your old one?"

I paused. "Fell in the lake," I said. At least he'd know why if Devon couldn't reach me.

"Oh, man, that sucks. Well, you gotta go all the way to Valley if you want it today. Otherwise, you order it online. There's nothing here in Sin-Pato, we're Sin-Phone Store too!"

★ ★ ★

I made it home just minutes before Carinna's truck pulled up. I checked the porch for any strange leavings, but the coast was clear. I fired up the computer and placed my cell-phone order. Jeez, not cheap. I was definitely going to make Scooter pay for it.

Not wanting any more surprises today, I had been listening for Carinna's truck—she didn't blast her horn, thankfully—and went out to meet her. She waved and jumped down, not quite as springy as August but impressive nonetheless.

We walked up the walkway together and went inside. I offered her something to drink. She took a glass of water. Her eyes were dilated. I guess she'd sampled her merchandise when she was at the monastery. I took out the Cambozola cheese that Devon and I had tackled last night, and her eyes lit up.

"That's good stuff," she said. I put out crackers and a cheese knife. She immediately slathered a cracker, nice and thick. "I tried to call you and let you know I was at the Duck Shop, see if you needed anything, but your phone was off," she said around the mouthful.

I edited the story. "I dropped it," I said. "It's now ringing at the bottom of No Duck Lake."

"Seriously? How did you get so close to the water?"

Um.

"I wanted to see what kinds of plants were growing there at the edge," I said. "It was in my pocket, I bent over, and in it went."

"Bummer," she said. "I was at the airport once, went to pee, my phone was in my back pocket, plop, right into the toilet."

"Before or after?"

She laughed and took another bite. "After, of course. So you want to head up to Cragstown?"

I was startled. "What for?"

"Well, to get a burner phone, of course. You can't get one here, and you don't want to go all the way to the phone store in Valley, forty-five minutes each way."

"Right, I ordered a new one online; it will be here Thursday. Sure, let's go up and get one. You know where?"

She eyed me. "Of course. I'll drive."

"You sure you're okay to drive all the way there?"

She grinned. "You noticed? I'm high about ninety-nine percent of my awake time, so I guess I'm okay." I still hesitated, but I wasn't sure the Prius was up to snuff. "Seriously, I'm good. I know my capacity, god knows."

★ ★ ★

Getting in Carinna's pickup truck was a lot easier than getting into August's truck. Carinna had a running board, which explained how she climbed in and out with such ease. "If the truck complains, we'll tell it to lump it!" she said. "So, I hear you're going to do your first Keeper duty tonight."

How did word get around so fast? "Yeah, just sort of a welcome evening, see how people react."

"Good for you. We've needed a new Keeper for so long. Your mom was a very cool lady, Sal."

"She was. Do you know how this Keeper business started? I mean, it's very, very strange, you know, to have a person who hears confessions—"

"Not confessions. Secrets. Things on people's minds. I don't know how it started. We should ask some of the older ladies; they would know. I think there was a Keeper before Alta, but that was before I was old enough to notice."

"I wish she were still around to ask," I said. It had been nearly a decade, and I didn't really miss her anymore, not actively anyway, but without the closure of really knowing what happened—even though we sat *shiva,* well, sort of informally, for my parents—there would always be this cloud on their deaths.

We were headed up the hill, using the Cragstown Road, the main route I had taken first. "Slow down up here," I said.

"Why? Is there a cop?"

"No, I want to show you something."

"Look who's the tour guide now!" But she slowed down. The development's story poles came into sight.

"Can you pull over at that sign?"

Carinna pulled the truck to a stop on the dusty shoulder. "Look," I said.

"Holy crap," she said. "Want to get out?" I nodded. We clambered out of the truck and went to look at the sign. She squinted in the sun. "It's the same developer," she said. "Pathways. I had no idea they were developing here too."

"I don't think it's *too*," I said. "It's *instead*."

"But what about the vineyard land? The land that Georgiana owned? Or co-owned? I don't know how that real estate stuff works. I just own my apartment buildings straight out, two of them I got when I was still married, nothing fancy. But we all knew that Georgiana was some part owner of the vineyard land, and that she was hot to get it developed. And no one in all of Simpato wanted that, but no one wanted to cross the Nose. She knew something about everyone. And I mean *everyone*."

"Even about you?" I asked.

She laughed. "Yep. But the things she thought would keep me in line were things I wasn't the least bit ashamed of. I didn't let her know that, so she wouldn't look for anything else."

So she wouldn't look for the real dirt.

We got back into the truck. Carinna seemed a lot more sober now.

"Do you know who else owns the vineyard land that you were talking about?" I asked. She must have some idea about the owners of other real estate in this very small town.

"It's something like THC," she said with a grin. "But it doesn't do anything for you. Kind of like when you buy creams or teas at the supermarket, and they have CBD in them instead of cannabis."

"What are you talking about?"

"You know, the stuff that's supposed to make your muscles feel—"

"No, I know what CBD is! What's it got to do with the development?"

She giggled. Maybe she wasn't okay to drive. "That's who owns the vineyard property with Georgiana. And I can't remember what it's called."

We drove on for a little while. "Do you mean an LLC?" I asked.

"That's it!"

"Any idea what else is in the name?" She shook her head, putting on her turn signal. "Asshat!" she muttered as the truck in the left lane sped past her. We had arrived in Cragstown.

Once again I was struck by how different it was from Simpato. "Welcome to Meth-town," Carinna said.

We drove past where I had turned, and soon a small downtown, not totally without charm, manifested in front of us. There were some shops, a couple of delis, an electronics store—"that's where we're going—" and a couple of gas stations. People on the street didn't look as scary as they had on the weekend.

"That's because during the week, people are working," she explained. "On the weekends, everyone clears out. There are lots of lakes and stuff for fishing, camping, some real natural beauty in Crags County, but not a lot for folks to do beyond that. And not too many jobs, either. Unless you work for the county itself, and this isn't even the county seat anymore. Used to be, back about forty years, but they moved it to the other side of the mountain, where you can connect up with the interstate easier and actually reach civilization."

She parked the truck in a little lot behind the store and we got out.

"The other thing," she said, "is that Cragstown is like, ninety-five percent white. Which is pretty noticeable, compared to Simpato, which is fifty-fifty. And if there are no Hispanics, it's because there's no place for people to work. Since a lot of Hispanics can't get things like disability, they can't just hang around places like Cragstown and do drugs. They go where the work is."

I wasn't inclined to get political, but I could see her point. "Seems there's plenty of work in Simpato."

"Yeah. Agriculture, wine, hotels, tourism, schools, the library. Speaking of the library, what did surfer-Scooter want with you this morning?"

I tensed up. "Nothing. He wanted to chat about me doing some literacy work like my mom did. The library's big on that." I was surprised at how easily that lie rolled off the tongue.

Carinna narrowed her green eyes at me. "Really? Okay, if you say so."

I guess the lie didn't really roll off that smoothly.

We entered the store. A thin man, in his late thirties or so, with a long light-brown mustache, stood behind the counter, a cigarette behind his ear. He wore sunglasses. Indoors. His right hand was drumming on the counter. His left hand was in a sling. "Ladies," he said when we approached the counter.

"She needs a burner," Carinna said.

"Does she?" he answered, and chuckled.

"A phone," I said.

"I know what you need," he said. He reached under the counter and took out a flip phone with charger. "Number gets activated when you put this in," he handed me a SIM card. "Good for a while. Toss it when you're done. Twenty bucks."

I reached for my wallet, pulled out a card.

He shook his head. "Nope, no cards. Don't want you to come crying to me if you use a credit card and your hubby finds you. Cash is king, baby."

CHAPTER TEN

We headed down the mountain. "Can we go the back way home?" I asked.

"Sure. Love the scenic route," Carinna said, turning off the main road.

I took out my new phone, opened it, and put the SIM card in. I hadn't had a flip phone since my first phone in high school. It had that way of texting where you had to push three times to get the letter you wanted.

"Takes me back to ninth grade," I said to Carinna. 'With that pain-in-the-neck texting. That's where all those abbreviations came from."

"Yeah. My first phone was like that too. I bought it with babysitting money. You know where the monastery is? Well, right behind it there used to be a playground, you know the kind, with a metal slide and that roundabout thing that you can break both legs on if you fall off, that kind. And a bunch of trees and tangles of bushes, and some falling-apart picnic tables.

"We used to go back there to smoke dope. I remember texting my boyfriend to meet me behind the nunnery, as we called it. NNRY was the abbreviation. I mean, that was what, maybe thirty-five years ago, but nothing changes here in Sin-Pato. We even had sex, well, not actual all-the-way but you know, duck action, close enough, back there a couple of times. About eight years ago they cleared it all out, paved it, gave it some modern play equipment and put in a bocce ball court ."

"That's too bad," I said, distracted by my phone. I was trying to remember Devon's number and send him a text.

"Yeah. Some shit went down back there maybe ten years ago, and the town decided that the high school kids were using it more than anyone else, for exactly what we were doing back in the day, so they bulldozed it."

I looked up. "Since you've been here forever, tell me about the nuns. How long has the nunnery, or the monastery or whatever been the Little Sisters of the Earth?"

"Oh, a good twenty years. Actually, when I was a kid it used to be an actual Catholic convent, and they ran a little preschool, and had that playground. But then it got harder and harder to find new nuns, I hear, so they shut it down, and then the Little Eco-Sisters came. Not twenty years, maybe fifteen years ago? They're not really nuns, you know."

"No?"

"Well, they're not Catholic nuns, which is the only kind I ever heard of. Sure they wear the habits, but most real nuns don't anymore."

"I wouldn't know. I'm Jewish."

"Yeah? Who knew. You're probably the only one in town!"

I ignored that. "So, they don't take vows of chastity and all that?"

"I don't know. Most of them aren't interested in men anyway. From what I've heard it's a refuge for climate-concerned Lesbians."

I looked over at her, wondering just how high she was. We were pulling into town already, at the far end of Peaches. "Have Marigold and Gingerroot been there long?" I asked.

"Nah, maybe a year. I'm not sure they're a good fit. I saw

that little Ginger giving Scooter the eye. Though who wouldn't, even if you usually liked girls. Funny," Carinna said, looking over at me.

"Watch the road," I said. "What's funny?"

"Oh yeah. Gingerroot, funny name for a nun, even these plant ladies. But funny that Marigold and Ginger came to Simpato not too long after Scooter came back."

"Back?" I'd heard part of the story from him, but it would be interesting to corroborate it.

"From Southern California where he went to school. He got into some kind of a jam and came back a bit over a year ago. Then a few months later, who joins the convent but Marigold and Gingerroot. A lot younger, a lot better looking than most of the nuns."

"And right around the time that the development of the vineyard got put back on the table," I added.

"Crazy, huh? And Scooter with that big scar under his jaw, and he sure won't be singing in the pageant anymore."

"He used to sing?"

Carinna laughed. "I'm an angel, so I guess it's no surprise he was the baby Jesus!"

★ ★ ★

Once again armed with a phone, I felt safer in the house after Carinna left. I tried again to remember Devon's cell, but I couldn't remember if the last three numbers were 535 or 353. I could just check my ph—no, damn. Amazing reflex.

At least Saul couldn't text me now, or not until tomorrow, anyway. Of course, there was always email, and I fired up my computer. Sure enough, another email from Saul. *We really need to talk*. Ok, I'll bite, I thought. *About what?*

Seconds later, the answer came. *Luna*.

Panicked, I grabbed the burner phone and punched in Saul's

number. No need to look that one up. It went to voicemail immediately. Of course. He didn't recognize the number. I considered emailing him my temporary number, and decided that email would have to do. Everything I found when I did a search for "burner phone" talked about avoiding the ex-husband/wife.

Phone broken, I emailed. *What about the cat?*

We'll have to talk. Tomorrow is okay, if you promise to pick up.

If you don't tell me what you're talking about, I won't promise. That's what's known as cat hardball. Like cat hairball, just messier. After all, he took Luna. That was real cat hardball. Like a custody battle when you don't have kids.

Suit yourself, he answered.

OK, I will. That's how adults behave. Take notes.

I looked at the time. It was nearly four. Devon hadn't shown up. Oh well. To distract myself from the vague disappointment that Devon had failed to materialize, I typed in Pathways Development into my search bar. A glossy website came up, "Bringing housing where people need it most." I flipped through the various webpages, looking for anything that resembled Cragstown or Simpato.

In their location search neither town came up. And yet they already had story poles up near Cragstown. I typed in *Coming Soon*. A completely black page came up, and slowly the center dissolved into a white dot, which became a small white duck. Then scrolling up from the bottom was the message, "Watch this space. Big news coming soon."

A duck, eh? I smiled. Either that was left over from when they'd planned to build in Simpato, or someone with an ironic sense of humor was playing on the fact that they were no longer building in "Without a Duck."

Probably neither. Developers weren't known for their funnybones.

I had meant to check the Secretary of State filing for

Pathways earlier. I quickly entered the information I knew into the official government search. What came up was information I already had. A typical LLC, and the agent—the person you'd serve if you were suing them—was some professional agent with an anodyne name and an address in Southern California. No other information was listed, even with an "advanced search."

On a whim I ran the name Georgiana Noyes. Well, well, well. She popped up as the registered agent of an LLC called SansCanard. Very funny. French for "without a duck." An advanced search yielded the information that the named Agent had been changed from a corporate entity, though not the same one as Pathways', to Georgiana herself. Significant? I didn't know enough about how LLCs ran to really understand whether the change mattered. It didn't mean that the manager had changed, I didn't think. I guess if I really wanted to understand it I could ask Saul, since this was his area, not mine. But I'd be damned if I would.

I glanced at my email. Brooks Campbell had answered my thank-you note, another charming and fully punctuated message inviting me to their home, for coffee or lunch sometime soon. Catherine just wasn't up to cooking anymore, otherwise they would have loved to invite me for dinner. Sweet people. I marked the email so I'd remember to respond later. Right now I had far too much going on.

It was still early enough for a walk to the monastery. I wondered what they'd be doing at this time. Not praying, I guess, if they weren't real nuns. Though my knowledge of what "real nuns" did could rattle in a tea cup.

Tea cup . . . Iced tea . . . I certainly wouldn't be taking refreshments there.

★ ★ ★

I walked up the four blocks to the monastery and found the big carved double-doors locked. I should have called ahead. There was a little side gate, about waist-high, and from the entrance I could see a path leading off around the building. The gate wasn't latched. I pushed it and entered.

The path led into a lush garden, with actual grass growing and olive trees in bud. The incipient leaves were too small to recognize on the other trees, but an olive tree stayed green, mostly, through the winter. There were benches and little chairs, a tiny stone table, and an archway with not-yet-budding grape vines climbing it. I stayed on the path as it curved around the building. From the rear of the structure I could now see the soaring front atrium's roof, as behind the massive frontage the building itself was a normal two-story wood-clad edifice.

I heard the sound of water and realized that the land backed up to the Valley River. A narrow gravel path, half as wide as the paved one I was on, led back to some trees, small and scrubby, natural-seeming rather than planted. I followed it to the brush, and the sound of the river was clear from there. Geographically, it must flow out of Simpato Lake, I thought. Maybe in twenty years my phone would turn up in these bushes.

I retraced my steps and once again continued on the paved path. It ran close to the back of the building, and windows with white curtains flashed in the afternoon light. Ahead was a Mexican-tile-paved patio that ran back all the way to a chain-link fence. The fence went from the street straight to the bushes, and presumably from there to the river. On the other side of the fence, little kids screeched on a teeter-totter, and a toddler was crying on the slide. His mother climbed up the three steps and brought him back down.

This was what Carinna had mentioned. All this patio, the bocce ball court, this modern playground, used to be trees and scrub, and the trysting place for the local Sin-Pato youth. No wonder they'd paved and patioed it.

"Can I help you?"

I jumped. I'd been so engrossed in my surroundings I'd forgotten that one, I was on private property, and two, I had come looking for Sister Marigold.

A green-clad nun was looking at me a little hostilely from a side door just ahead.

"I'm sorry, Sister."

"Don't *sister* me. Who are you and what are you doing back here?" Not exactly the friendly reception I'd gotten from everyone else. "Wait. I recognize you. You're that Keeper nonsense. Here to take confession, huh?" I could hear that she said *nonsense* so as to not say *bullshit*. I was offended, even though I sort of thought of it the same way. After all, I hadn't chosen the role.

"Some have greatness thrust upon them," I said with a shrug.

To my surprise, she laughed. "Good one. Sorry. What brings you here?"

I wondered what caused the sudden shift until l saw another wimple appear in the window, this one much lower. Sister Sorghum or Mother Sassafras, no doubt. "I'm here to see Sister Marigold, but the front door was locked."

"Certainly. I'll fetch her," the nun said, not inviting me in. "You may wait in the garden. Lemonade or a cookie?" I shook my head, but she was gone, shutting the door and, from the sound of it, locking it behind her.

I went back to the little benches. The sun was streaming down on this west side of the building, and it was beautiful and peaceful.

The peace was shattered by Sister Marigold appearing from the side, and behind her, the first nun, scolding her vigorously, and carrying two glasses—of etched glass, exactly like the ones that had been left on my doorstep—of lemonade and a plate of cookies on a tray. "When I say you offer refreshments, Sister," she said, dragging out each S, "you serve refreshments. You're here to obey, not invent your own rules! Sorry," she said, turning to me, "youngsters take a while to learn the ropes." The nun set the tray down on the little stone table with a bang.

"I'll be just inside if you need anything," she said and started to flap away.

"Thanks? Sister . . ."

She turned back. "Right. Sister Ephedra."

"Thank you, Sister," I said. *Ephedra.* As a person named Salvia, I couldn't help but know that Ephedra was the source of natural ephedrine, the closest thing to amphetamines in the American natural plant world.

"What a pill," Marigold said. "Thinks she's the next Mother Superior. Not that Sassafras is going anywhere. But thanks for coming," she added. "I was hoping to speak with you on Saturday, but things sure went sideways, didn't they?"

I wondered how much she knew. "Poor Ms. Noyes," I said. That seemed safe. I mean, the woman had died, so any pity was well-placed.

"Bitch deserved what she got," Marigold said. "Cookie?"

I was speechless, a condition so rare with me that I feared I was having a ministroke. "No thanks," I finally croaked out.

"They're the plain kind," she assured me, broke one in half, and took a bite. She made a face and spat it out. "They're supposed to be. Damned Ephedra."

A lot to take in, in less than a minute—the etched glasses, which led to the obvious question of which of the Sisters had left them for me; a nun who would provide laced cookies when plain ones were expected; and a nun who called a recently deceased local townswoman a bitch, then cursed a fellow nun. "You a real nun?" I asked.

She laughed out loud. Not the text acronym, but a real, throaty laugh. "Caught me. No, I'm a journalist. Independent. Researching a long piece on commission for"—she named a very, very prominent magazine—"and Mother Sassafras is the only one who knows, so keep it under your hat, so to speak."

I digested that bit of news. "What's the story you're after?" She hesitated. "Look, despite your comment at the service, or whatever that's called, I *am* extraordinarily good at keeping secrets."

She at least looked a bit embarrassed. "Oh, that. That was just theater. Of course you're as trustworthy as anyone else. But it led to something very interesting. Would you like to come up to my room? I have something to show you."

I will admit I hesitated. First Scooter, now Marigold. "What's your real name?" I asked.

"Margo Schwartz."

I smiled. "I'm originally Salvia Grossman." I got up. "Let's go see what you have to show me." Call it tribalism, call it what you will, I was happy to find a fellow Jew in the Sin-Jewish-Ducks city.

We went in the small side door, right into a beautifully appointed kitchen. Every modern convenience sat on the gleaming black stone countertops, the floor looked as clean as a floor-wax commercial set, and copper pans gave a warm light across lemony walls. "Wow," I said.

"Right?"

Marigold led me down a long hallway with doors every ten feet. Most doors were closed, with small framed flower or leaf paintings on each one. "Name plates," she said. A couple of doors were ajar, and inside I saw white walls, few adornments, white-curtained windows. We stopped at a door with a marigold. "The doors don't lock," she said, opening hers. "Not much privacy when you're a nun."

Inside her room was the same narrow single bed I'd seen in the others, a desk—this one with an up-to-date Apple laptop, a printer, a wifi booster, a lamp, and a metal box with a lock. "I guess you make your own privacy," I said.

She pulled a key from her robe, opened the box, and took out a folded piece of paper. "Have a seat," she said, indicating the foot of the bed. I sat, and she sat down next to me. "Take a look."

The paper was plain white computer paper, and written in loopy modern high-school-girl handwriting was a note *Mari, I've got to get out of here. Don't tell Sass til lunch. I can't do it anymore. You have my number. Xxoo Ginger.*

"She left?" Marigold nodded. "Did she know who you were?"

"Not really. We were paired together a lot. She was always nervous. I mean, she guessed I wasn't going to make it as a nun, any more than she was. But we were treated as novices, and she figured I was going to wash out of the program, and it was clear from early on that she was too. You do know that most of the nuns here are gay, right?"

I nodded. Thanks to Carinna I did.

"I'm not," Marigold continued. "And Ginger isn't either. That's her real name, you know. It's actually Virginia, but she always went by Ginger. Nice and old-fashioned. She's from Fresno." Fresno, home of the Bulldogs, a city in the Central Valley of California known for an intense winter fog that rose from the ground, obliterating roads, and as a halfway pitstop on Highway 99. Not exactly cutting-edge.

"So Ginger left," I prodded.

"She ran away on Sunday morning. No one has seen or heard from her since."

That made three: Georgiana, who of course was found; the mayor, who wasn't found yet; and now Ginger. "Did you tell the police?"

"No. And I'm not going to act dumb and exclaim *The police? Why would we tell the police?* I know perfectly well that Noyes the Nose was murdered." At my look she added, "Doesn't take a rocket scientist. She leaves here, goes up the mountain in her town clothes, no hiking shoes, dies, and it's all hush-hush. If she'd just fallen, well, that would just show her stupidity. If she'd had a stroke or something, that would be in her obit. As it was, no one is talking. Obviously, something is fishy. And the mayor? Mister big-secret? Gone too. Put two and two together."

That didn't sound very journalistic to me. Or at least, what we used to think of as journalistic. I considered telling her that the police were concerned about Mayor Solis, but I was troubled by her demeanor.

"Okay, since I don't know the players well, and you seem to, do you think that the mayor had something to do with Noyes's death?"

She sighed. "I don't know. But someone did her in. I didn't think much of Georgiana Noyes's columns, but she was great at ferreting out gossip. And I was always worried that she would figure me out as well. At least she hadn't up until she died. But I'm good at figuring things out too, and it seemed that she had a big financial interest in the property that was going to be developed. She and that LLC, Anatra Land."

The name rang a bell, but I couldn't place it. I was definitely not going to tell Marigold about SansCanard. But she was still talking.

"And the mayor opposed the development, because he has a property up near Cragstown, and he and Cragstown's mayor were in cahoots to get Pathways to develop up there. So he threw every possible roadblock in the way of the vineyard development. And he planned a big announcement, so who the hell knows."

Some nun she was. "And Ginger?"

Marigold shook her head. "Oh, she had nothing to do with any of that. Ginger came to the Little Sisters after she got knocked up in Fresno. Her parents wouldn't let her have an abortion. They're not like Coastal Californians down there in the Central Valley, trust me. She came up here to have the baby. She hadn't decided if she would keep it or give it up, she wasn't that far along. Most places it would have been no big deal either to have an abortion or to be a single mom, but her parents were big in their church, and she wasn't eighteen yet. So they sent her up here. She, um, lost the pregnancy within a week of getting here."

Uh huh.

"I would have too," Marigold said. "But then she decided she didn't want to go back to Fresno, and she asked if she could join the Sisters. They were delighted. I don't think they've had anyone under thirty in—ever. Of course, they aren't real nuns, so that helps."

"I suppose. And then she changed her mind?"

Marigold nodded. "She's eighteen now, so she can do what she wants. Her parents think she's here waiting for the baby."

"Won't they be surprised," I said. "I guess that was eating at her?"

"Yeah, that and she was afraid that the Nose would say something about her and the baby—or lack of baby—in her column. I told her she wasn't important enough."

I raised an eyebrow.

"In a nice way. But then she met the librarian. Have you met Scooter?" I nodded. "Real head-turner if you like the Endless Summer look. She started sneaking out at night. I tried to cover for her, but she got caught with him in her room on Saturday. He has a nice body, scar and all. Trust me, I've seen it."

Oh.

"She didn't run away with him," I said. "I've seen him twice since. He's not a nice guy."

"No shit," said the pseudo-nun. "Hell of a good lay, but definitely not nice."

"What did the nuns do when they caught her?"

"That's the thing. They told her that she'd be punished, have to clean all the bathrooms or something on Monday, and for now she could just repent. Probably because when they caught her, she and Scooter were just talking in her room. She was fully dressed, apparently. But I'm worried anyway. Someone might think she left because she knew something about the Nose or the mayor. So what do you think we should do?"

I thought a moment. "Why are you asking me?" I finally said.

She looked surprised. "Oh. Obviously. First, you're a lawyer so you'll probably think clearly."

I smiled. "So first being a lawyer makes me untrustworthy, and now it makes me a clear thinker?" I thought of Saul. Well, that was clear thinking, if not honest doing.

"Second," she was saying, "you're older, probably wiser, and are definitely calmer than the rest of the town. And third, you're hanging out with the Chief of Police, so you can probably just tell him, you know, pillow-talk."

"Jesus, Margo!" I said. "I'm not sleeping with Devon!" She *was* good at finding gossip, wasn't she? And extremely willing to jump to unsupported conclusions.

"Devon, is it?" she grinned.

"You know, for a journalist you sure don't double-check things, do you? You get what you think are your facts and draw some pretty wild inferences. But I guess I need to check my idealism at the door." I was furious.

"Well said, for a disbarred lawyer."

The gloves were off.

"Suspended, with only seven weeks left. It's public record, so it's not as if you can use it to blackmail me—if that's what passes for journalism these days."

She smiled tightly. "Not so, Salvia. Who's going to trust a Keeper who's been suspended for fraud?"

I smiled back, just as tightly. "So then I'm not the Keeper. Didn't want to be in the first place. And Scooter found out before you did. Besides, your story won't get written once everyone knows you're a journalist. Who sleeps with subjects. And doesn't bother to look behind the superficial, either."

We both stared at each other. Then I shook my head. "Welcome to middle-school. Without a Duck."

She started to laugh. And then so did I. Neither of us had had any cookies, either. "This is stupid," I said.

"You're right. I'm sorry."

"Same," I said. "I'll tell Devon about Ginger tonight. I hope she's okay."

"As long as that Scooter doesn't have her tied up in his basement or something."

★ ★ ★

It was getting close to five, and I was expected to hold my first Keeper's hours in about ten minutes. Devon, no surprise, had never shown up. It was a test, in my mind. If he felt exposed or vulnerable—heaven forfend that I should use such terms about a man and the Chief of Police, no less—and couldn't visit as promised, then his emotional unavailability was something I didn't need. For that, I could—-

I stopped myself. What on earth was I doing, *relationshipizing* someone I'd only met five days ago, in an official capacity no less? I'd been divorced officially for a month now. Was I so programmed that I needed a relationship with a man all the time?

Disgusted with myself, I went to my deck and arranged the Brown Jordan chairs in an inviting way. Would I need refreshments? I didn't think so, no one had mentioned anything, but perhaps some ice water and paper cups to wet the dry throats of my confessional visitors? I certainly wasn't going to serve pot brownies.

I ran the water into a pitcher, put some cubes in it, and found a sleeve of paper cups in a cabinet. I had brought them for my first few days, thinking it would take me longer to unpack than it did. What else?

Whatever else I might have served was rendered moot by the

arrival of a group of four women probably in their fifties, one in orange stretch pants that she'd clearly bought when she'd been their size and that now had to do extra duty around the back. It was eye-catching, in the sense that underwear visible through pants always is. The rest were more conventionally dressed in jeans or sweatpants with long t-shirts or sweatshirts, and one wore a FortyNiners cap.

They stopped at the edge of the first deck. They waited, looking at me expectantly. Was I supposed to do something? Say something?

"Hi," I tried. They backed up a bit. "Would you like to come up?"

They exchanged looks but didn't come forward.

The decks were built by my dad in the early days of their owning the house, and were terraced down from the kitchen door to the unpaved area just before the end of the driveway. August had taken the distance in four steps, but for most it would take a walk of five or six steps for the first deck and another four across the second, ending in a wide step in front of the kitchen door. The four women were huddled at this point on the edge of the dirt area, nearly stepping back onto the drive.

I looked at my watch. Five on the nose.

The thought of the Nose brought me up short for a moment. I was expected to report anything I heard about her, or the mayor, to the police. I wondered if anyone would say anything.

If they didn't want to come up, and didn't want to talk, just gawk at me, so be it. I sat down in one of the chairs, poured myself a glass of water, and leaned back.

Another group of women arrived at the driveway and made their way partway up. They were younger, with long dark hair in various extensive braids or ponytails. They too, stopped and waited.

I put my cup of water down on the side table. Maybe . . .

I poured a second cup and put it near the other chair. One woman from the group moved expectantly, so the water was clearly a part of the ritual. But with everyone staring at me like that, there would be no privacy for anyone to come up.

I stood up and reversed my chair, facing away from the group. Then I reversed the other chair as well, so if anyone came up we'd have our backs to the group.

There was a palpable exhale, and one woman from the first group came walking up the deck. Lucky guess.

She was definitely past fifty on closer examination, and she was wearing a striped top that made her look like a round referee. Her short hair was gray and curled, and her glasses were slightly smudged. I wanted to reach over and take them and clean them.

Maybe instead of Secret Keeper I could be Glasses Cleaner.

"Hi," she said. "You look a lot like your mom."

"Thanks," I said, thinking that I didn't really, but it was a nice thing to say. "My name is Sal. I know my mom did this, this Keeper thing, but I'm not quite sure how to go about it."

"That was pretty obvious," she said, but she said it kindly. "I'm Sandra, I live about three blocks from here. Me and my friends, we just wanted to say hello, see how you were going to do this."

"Can they come up too, or is that not the way?"

"Oh, if I was going to tell you something, they shouldn't because, you know, privacy, but since we're just saying hi, that would be okay." She turned to the other three, who were watching us intensely, and waved them up.

"Cara," said the first, panting slightly from the journey across the decks.

"Michelle."

"Andie," said the woman in the orange pants.

"Nice to meet you all. I'm Sal."

"We know."

"How do I go about doing this?" I asked.

Andie giggled. "You got it more or less," she said. "You sit down, turn your back, and the first person comes up. They don't get to stay more than about five minutes. If they go on too long, you say, 'that's as much as I can Keep.' And they leave, and the next person comes up."

"Sounds pretty straightforward. And all I have to do is keep their secrets? I don't have to give advice?"

"God no!" Sandra said. "No advice. Just listen. Pat some hands, say *there, there,* have some tissues, water's good, you got that. Some folks have no one to listen to them. We have each other, but still, it's good to have an outside person to tell."

"And after two hours, you turn your chair back around, and you're done. Even if folks are waiting. They can come back next week, or whenever your next day is."

"How do people know what days I'm doing it?"

Sandra leaned in. "We haven't had a Keeper since your mom, um, passed away." The four crossed themselves. A murmur came up from the younger women waiting, and then I heard male murmurs too. I didn't dare glance around to see who was waiting.

"Yeah, that was before the Nose. But you could put it in the *Quack.* Or on Facebook. The WAD."

"Rest in peace," said one, and I couldn't tell which, because at that point the sound of a pickup roaring up the drive drowned her out. The four put their hands on their ears. A blast of a horn announced August's arrival.

The four women left, patting my shoulder and wishing me well. As soon as they were off the deck, one of the younger women, with a plait as wide as my forearm and just as long, stepped up. She looked about twenty, but it was harder and harder to guess younger folks' age. "Hi," she said. "Can I tell you a secret?" I nodded. "I'm pregnant."

I took a deep breath. If this girl had no one else to tell . . . I patted her hand. "How do you feel about that?" I asked.

"Um, okay," she said. She seemed a little surprised. I smiled. "And I think the father is going to be happy."

I nodded. "Good. Eat healthy and get your checkups, okay?"

Again she seemed a little taken aback. I wasn't supposed to give advice. But twenty years as a lawyer made a certain amount of that instinctive.

"Anything else?" I said.

"Nuh. I'm just glad we've got a Keeper again. I thought I was going to burst with the secret. I feel better."

"Good. Well, take care," I said. She nodded, stood up. "And come back again, let me know how it's going."

She smiled a bit. "Just getting the hang of it, aren't you? Well, you're doing good. We need you." And she skipped down the steps to the drive. "*Hola, Augustín*," she said. Ah. So that's why August was named August.

The next person to approach was no surprise. Folding his long legs into the chair was Scooter. I knew, somehow, he wouldn't miss this opportunity. I wondered if I dared ask him if he knew where Ginger was.

He stretched out in the seat. "So, ready for a secret?"

"Maybe. Depends on what it is."

"That's not how the Keeper acts," he said, but he was smiling. He poured himself a cup of water, raised the cup in a mock cheer, and drank. "I know where the mayor is."

"Do you?" I said mildly. "Tell all."

"That's more like it. So how do I know you won't rat me out?"

"You don't, I guess. Ever talk to my mom?"

He went silent, and I could see the switch flipping. I tensed. He took a breath, shuddered it under control. "What did she tell you?"

"Nothing! I never even knew that she was doing this!"

"Bullshit, Sal. What. Did. She—"

"Hey, hey, Scooter!" We both jumped. Sergio, still in uniform, trotted up the steps. "How's it going, bro?" He put out his hand sideways for a bro-shake.

Scooter stood up. "Sergio." He was again the cool senior talking down to a sophomore hanger-on. "What's shaking?" He was walking down the steps as he spoke. Sergio turned and watch him go.

"Guy never changes, you know? Even after he went through rehab and got clean, he's still the same dude he was at Duck. Too cool for school, you know what I'm saying?" But he looked crestfallen. Even his uniform hadn't gotten him in with the top crowd. "Everything going okay? Folks being nice to you?"

I nodded. He had just spoiled a chance for me to get some real information. I wondered, was even the fact that Scooter knew, or claimed to know, where the mayor was a secret? Whether it was or wasn't, I would tell Devon when he went on duty tonight.

Even if he hadn't come to see me like he said he would, he was the chief. He needed to know.

"Okay, well if everything's cool, I'll take off," Sergio was saying.

"Yeah, I'm good," I said. Though if Scooter came back after Sergio left, I might not be. "Stop by again if you feel like it," I said.

"Hey, five minutes!"

I turned around and saw August, bouncing up and down at the edge of the deck. There was no one else waiting.

"Keep your pants on, August," Sergio said. "Or I'll run you in."

August stepped back. For him, I guess, the uniform mattered, even if they were friends. I remembered Carinna saying that long ago August had briefly been arrested for the murder of the real estate agent. A guy like that could be scarred for life. And Sergio was casually using it for status.

"See you, Sergio," I said. "Thanks for stopping by."

"No prob," he said. "I'll let the chief know I saw you and all was well."

He punched August in the shoulder as he went by. "Be a Duck," he said.

August's step had lost its bounce when he came the rest of the way up the deck. "Hey, Sally. What a twinkie that guy always was. Trying to hang with the older guys, always saying the stupid thing. Even now, if we go for a beer, as soon as someone he knows comes into the bar, he's like, I don't know, like he would love to whip out his badge and show off."

I knew guys like that, and girls too. "Strivers," I said. "That's what people who do that are called."

"Strivers," August repeated. "You're teaching me great words. So, ready for a secret?" That seemed to be the formula. I poured him a cup of water. "I think this is an important secret, Sally." I didn't correct him. It was his time. "Really important."

"Okay," I said slowly. "Go ahead, I'm listening."

"Um. So. Okay, so I told your mom, before she left, about this. But there's more."

I waited.

"When I was in high school, I got arrested." I nodded. He didn't know I knew that. "But that's not the secret because I think everyone knows. But it wasn't me. Everyone knows that too, I think. And I knew who did it. But I didn't tell."

There was a lot of *thinks* in there for a guy who supposedly didn't do a lot of thinking. I nodded. "Go on."

"Because that poor kid didn't have a mom. And my mom always helped me, and he had no one to help him grow up right. He . . . he," August swallowed. "He had a dad. But he was an asshole. Sorry, Sally. I mean, they both were. Him and his dad. But his dad was way, way worse. So I didn't tell anyone, except your mom. And then they let me out."

Oh my.

"But that's not my secret, I mean, that secret I already told your mom, so it's done, right?"

I nodded. Holy mackerel.

"But my secret is, he's back. He came back. And I saw him again, in Cragstown. He didn't see me, I don't think. But I need to tell someone."

"Wow," I said. "How do you feel about that?" It was the right question with the pregnant girl. Maybe it would be with August too.

"Scared. I'm super scared. I know he did it. Scooter knows he did it, too, but him and Scooter were friends. I mean, we all were, only me and Scooter know. He was gone for a while, just like Scooter, but now he's back."

CHAPTER ELEVEN

At seven I turned my chair to face the driveway. There were two guys in jeans and workboots still waiting. It seemed folks brought friends with them, but only the giver of the secret would come forward.

"I can take one more, if you'd like." I felt bad leaving the last group burdened.

"Uh, great," said one of the guys, a bearded fellow with a dirty cap on backward.

I turned the chair around again, and he came up the steps, his boots making the wood shake. He sat down, I poured him a cup of water, and he took a long sip.

"Welcome back," he said.

"Thanks. I'm not my mom, but I am glad to be here to listen to your secret."

He looked over at me. His bushy eyebrows were knitted. "I know you." I shook my head. "No, really. Not recently. But a long time ago, maybe fifteen years ago, you used to visit with your boyfriend or whatever."

"Husband."

"Okay. But I saw you recently. I'm great with faces. Never ever forget one once I've seen—holy shit! You're the lady that found the dead one on the mountain!"

I froze. "I'm one of the ladies that was hiking there, and we came across that poor woman in the cave. Were you, um, one of the first responders?"

I was hoping. I was especially hoping that he wasn't the one who killed her. *That* would be a secret I'd go right to the station with. I made myself look at him. I wasn't particularly good with faces, myself, but if I put my mind to it I'd remember more than the eyebrows and the smell. Smells were like an imprint to me, but I couldn't imagine going through a lineup at the police station sniffing the potential defendants.

He cleared his throat. "That's my secret, that I wanted to tell you. Like I said, I never forget a face. Names, no, I suck at them."

No, that couldn't be his secret, since he supposedly just recognized me. I waited. *Beard, bushy eyebrows, thin, workman's attire, greenish-hazel eyes, broken front tooth . . .*

"Okay, I'm ready to hear your secret."

He paused. "But since you were there . . ." I waited. Like a good lawyer, I knew people generally talked to fill a silence. He took a deep breath, then exhaled cigarette-tinged breath. "There was a guy that came up the mountain with her. I was, um, I was walking up there, I, shit. Okay. Here goes. There was a guy who came up the mountain. I seen him before, he's from here, looks like a surfer dude, he came up with her, and she was acting really strange, she was crying, and she took off her shirt, not like they were going to fuck or anything, excuse me, ma'am, it wasn't like that, more like she was upset and tore her top or something. She was kind of like fighting herself. I dunno . . . I can't get the words right."

"It's okay," I said gently. "Just say what you see in your brain. Don't worry about the words."

He closed his eyes. "So the guy, the surfer, he's like, he started laughing. I couldn't hear what they were saying but he was, like, egging her on. I didn't like how it all looked, and I was going to go tell him to back off, you don't treat a lady like that, when I don't know if he saw me or what, but he turned around and ran down the hill. And let me tell you, he ran like, you know, a deer or something. I never saw anyone run so, like an animal. Like he was born running."

I knew who he meant. I just nodded.

"Then there was another guy, he came from the path around the mountain. I only saw him from the back, or I'd be able to remember him. I only got a glimpse; he was wearing a plaid shirt. I was worried about the broad. And the next thing I know, *she's* gone. I'm sure she didn't go down the hill. She must of gone into the cave where she died. I don't know. Then I heard some females talking, and you and the White Lady came up, so I took off."

We both exhaled hard. My heart was so loud I nearly didn't hear what he said. Nearly. "So I took her shirt and hung it on a bush. I didn't know where she'd gone, but if she came back looking for it, I wanted her to find it. And I left by the other path and went home."

I nodded. My hands were shaking when I reached for my water cup. "Okay," I said. "Thanks for your secret."

He nodded.

"Glad we have a Keeper again. I would have burst keeping that one."

★ ★ ★

The sun had set, it had turned cold, and I was glad to be inside. I had so much to digest from my first round as a Keeper. How did my mother stand it for all those years?

I was making tea when an old Jeep pulled into my drive. I could see Devon through the open side. So he didn't drive a pickup truck or a BMW, the two choices in Simpato. I looked at my watch. Seven thirty. I suppose that counted as stopping by. I wondered if this was a social call or a check-in, but either way I had a lot to report.

I paused mentally. People had trusted me. They believed that their secrets were safe with me. Of course, there was also a murder, a missing man, and a departed, though possibly voluntarily, young woman. All of that pointed to necessity, a damned good reason to breach any confidences.

He knocked on the kitchen door, then opened it. That was overly familiar, I thought.

"Hey. Good to see you're alive," he said.

"Likewise," I answered. "Why wouldn't I be. Oh! Unless you got my—wait, just tell me why you said that."

"Can I come in?"

"You're more than halfway there. Tea? Wine?"

"Water would be great. I'm going on duty at eight. I was supposed to be off today but—"

"Right. The guy from the sheriff's office didn't show up. Sergio told me."

Devon relaxed. "Good, so you knew. But where have you been? I tried to text you a bunch of times, got one answer saying you had notifications silenced, and then nothing after that."

"Did you get my text with the photo from Mount Santabella?"

"No! What were you doing up on the mountain? There's a murderer out there, Sal!"

"I guess you'd better sit down. I've got a lot to report."

I took my tea to the living room, and he followed with his glass of water. Seemed pretty inhospitable of me, but he sure couldn't have wine if he was going to work. Nothing like the Chief of Police with wine on his breath.

"Me too," he said. "I've got some information to share with you too. But I couldn't text it, that's for sure, it's not something that will be public for a while. I wanted to come by earlier, but my son, Alex, had a crisis today, took up my entire afternoon."

He shook his head. Being childless myself, I didn't know

if I should ask or just nod sympathetically. It's not like I could give advice, unless he was thinking of changing his will or something. I went with nodding. I'd perfected that over the last two hours.

"He wants to give up theater. It's his whole life, he's going to school just for that, and he's thinking of giving it up."

"That doesn't sound so bad. After all, unless he's going to take up poetry or something that pays even less, maybe he'll choose something that he can actually earn a living wage at."

Devon's mouth narrowed to a line. "I gave up my dream because I was becoming a father at twenty. He doesn't have to give up his dream. Plenty of actors make a decent living."

"Waiting tables. Nannying. Not acting. That's a pyramid with a very, very narrow top."

"At his age it isn't about making money. It's about following his dream. His passion. And now he wants to give it up, drop out of Oregon State, and . . ." He put his head down. "I know, Sal. It's his life. He can make mistakes. But I know him better than he knows himself. He can do anything he wants after college, but this is the one thing that makes him happy."

I let him breathe through it. It was *his* dream that was being given up. "Look, Devon. I don't have kids, so I've got no right to an opinion, but it's his life. And he can always go back to it. Maybe a semester off might do him some good. What did he say he wants to do instead?"

Devon shook his head. "He wants to go to India, for crying out loud. Study with some kind of guru. And, get this. He wants to become a school crisis counselor. I'd be proud, but I'm just so blown away. And of course, being the drama queen that he is, this all involved a million phone calls, crying, threats, involving his mother, involving damned Steve, oh god, what a day."

"Too bad you're going to work," I said. "You need something stronger than water. But look, you've got to put all that aside.

We've got information to share, and you've got to be at the station in ten minutes. You first, then I'll fill you in. After all, I can always tell you at the station."

He smiled forlornly. "Yeah. I shouldn't be telling you anything, so if I'm going to, I'd better do it here. Now that I've spilled my guts again. You're a born Keeper, Sal."

"Just wait. You have no idea. Now, spill the rest of the tea."

"Georgiana had drugs in her system. Methamphetamine, to be exact."

"Oh god, really? She was into that?"

He shook his head. "No. Apparently, the lab and autopsy reports say that she wasn't a regular user. It changes you. Rots your teeth, screws up your system. It looks like she ingested it somehow, there were traces in her stomach—this is gross, stop me if you're squeamish."

"I'm not. I do wills and estates. My work only gets interesting when someone dies. I'm good."

"So she ate something with meth in it. There were the remnants of a cookie, like from the monastery, but it didn't show any contamination. It was straight oatmeal cookie. There was her breakfast. But in the liquid contents, sorry Sal, of the stomach there was meth. So maybe she drank it. Or what I mean is, it was in something she drank. And the last place she was before she went up the mountain was the monastery."

"Wow," I said. I thought of the lemonade and cookies served to me today. And how the cookie was laced with cannabis, when it wasn't supposed to be. I shuddered. Plus, that was today?

"There may not be any crime in Simpato," I said, "but there are sure a lot of very strange and bad things going on. Let's see, where to begin . . ."

Devon looked at his watch. "Damn, got to go. Can you come down to the station? We can talk there."

"Formal request?"

He smiled. "Sure. Formal request. Get something to eat if you haven't already, and come down as soon as you can."

★ ★ ★

I took Devon's advice and boiled up some ravioli and sauce. I eyed the Chenin Blanc, decided against it. Liquid courage was overrated, made me stupid, and I couldn't afford to be stupid right now. As it was, every breeze, every squirrel, every sound made me jump. I opened my computer while I ate. There was another plaintive note from Saul—what on earth did he want?—and the auto-reminder that I hadn't responded to Brooks Campbell's email. I typed him a short note. *Coffee tomorrow?* I could bring some snacks if it suited him and Catherine. Not a minute later he sent me an enthusiastic *Yes!* And his address. It would make a nice respite from these sordid adventures.

I grabbed the burner phone, my wallet, and a jacket. I locked the front door, went out the back, and locked the back door. As I did it, I recited a mantra: *I am keeping myself safe; I am not being paranoid; I am not the target of this crap.*

I started the Prius. It moaned, unhappy to be woken from its long slumber. We were only going a few blocks, I said. I just didn't want to walk back. It started, then quietly stopped. "You aren't supposed to break, ever!" I said to it. It didn't even answer. "Fine. We'll get you to a mechanic. It's a good thing I didn't try to drive you to Cragstown today."

The car didn't even try to appear chastened. It sat there like a lump of metal motor vehicle. "Suit yourself," I said, getting out. I slammed the door and walked down the drive. Really, it was only four blocks to the station. "Lump it," I said over my shoulder. The Prius flashed its lights back at me as I hit the lock button on the key.

At the station, to my surprise, Devon was sitting at the reception desk. "Demoted?" I asked.

He chuckled. "Needs must. Night guys are out on calls, I need to be at the desk. Grab one of those chairs, no, here, I'll get one for you." He pulled a folding metal chair up across from his chair. "Sorry, not the most comfortable."

I sat. "It doesn't matter. But let's get down to business. I have a lot to tell you. You sure we can't go into an interview room? I wouldn't want anyone to come in and see me talking to you."

"That bad, huh? Reputation at risk?" he smiled.

"Actually, yes. But in the sense of being the Keeper. Not my, um, personal . . ." I felt myself blush.

"I understand. But no, we have to be out here. I'll look stern, though. Like you have to be here. You try to look uncomfortable."

Once I started, I wouldn't be faking it.

"To begin with, the reason you couldn't reach me all day is because Scooter made me go walking with him on the mountain, and he took my phone away from me and threw it in the lake."

After I scraped Devon off the ceiling, he calmed down. But I understood. The more I thought about it, the more frightening it became.

"Do you know what happened to him in Southern California, before he came back?" I asked.

He shook his head. "Scooter left before my time. A few months after the murder of the real- estate agent, he went to college in Santa Barbara and stayed. Then he came back last year. So I don't know all that much."

"I think you may need to find out. Can you ask Carinna? I think she knows."

"Our local pot seller? Karen Monarch?"

"That's her real name? Yeah. She knows everything about Sin-Pato. As does August."

"August sometimes talks to Sergio, but you might have noticed that August isn't the sharpest tool in the shed. And

Sergio, well, he's a mixed bag. He'll be a good cop one day, but he's still full of himself over his badge. Usually it's the school bullies who become cops, but now and then it's their victims, and that's what we have here."

"Even the high-school girls still ignore him," I said.

"So tell me what happened with your Keeper session." I hesitated. "Look, Sal, this whole Keeper business is bizarre, I agree. But it isn't a legal secret. You're not there as their lawyer. And if a life hangs in the balance . . ."

"Even a lawyer has to say something. I know. It's just, okay. Here goes. First, Scooter showed up."

"Wait, what? That bastard is really skirting the edge of getting himself arrested."

"Listen. It isn't what he told me, because he didn't tell me anything. It's the dynamic. When Sergio turned up to check on me, Scooter left. But as he passed Sergio, he kind of lorded it over him like they were still in high school, when Scooter was a popular guy. And Sergio was a dweeb wannabe hanger-on. Younger and totally not cool. Sergio resented it.

"Then a few benign visits, an older group of ladies, a girl with a bun in the oven—"

"Haven't heard that expression in a while," Devon said.

"Still happens. In fact, before I even did the Keeper thing, but *after* I went up on the mountain with Scooter and went to Cragstown with Carinna to get a burner phone—"

"Jesus Christ! You've been busy! Sorry about the swearing."

"It isn't a swear-word to me," I smiled.

"Right."

"Anyway, I can't believe how long this day's been. Should I tell you about going to the monastery? Or continue on the Keeper?"

"Depends on what's more important," Devon said. "But let's finish the Keeper first."

"Okay. This is the important stuff: Scooter knows where the mayor is."

"I know. I had him in yesterday for a short conversation. He's so jumpy it was very short. He said he thought that the mayor was in Cragstown, not dead. He also suggested that we look a little deeper into the monastery—the Little Sisters have something up their sleeves. Which correlates with what we found, sort of, in poor Georgiana's system. And makes me very interested in what you found there. But finish the Keeper first."

"Okay. So you know Scooter knows where the mayor is. But he knows something more and didn't get a chance to tell me. But then August came. August knows who killed someone about ten years ago, I'm guessing that's the real estate guy, and says that Scooter knows too, and that the guy who did it is back."

Devon's eyes were wide. "Holy mackerel," he finally breathed. "That's quite a harvest."

"Yeah. August said he was first arrested for the murder, but then my mother apparently knew he hadn't done it, and then they let August go, which implies, of course, that my mom went and told a secret."

"I wasn't there, Sal. But that's the word."

We were quiet for a bit. "And then a few months later, they decided to sail to Hawai'i, in March, and were not seen since. Without telling me and my sister. Devon, if that's connected . . ."

He put his hand out, hesitated, then put it on my arm. "We don't know that, Sal. We may never know. Let's stay in the present. What else happened at the Keeper session?"

I was still in the past. I felt tears welling up. I pulled my arm away gently. Just in time, too. The door to the police station swung open, and the night shift strode in.

"About time, Billy," Devon said.

"Got stuck in my last shift, took effing forever to get over the mountain to Simpato."

"Sal, this is Billy Peale, from the Sheriff's department. He's taking an extra eight tonight to keep Simpato safe. Billy, this is Sal DeVine, new resident, daughter of Alta and Stan Grossman, formerly of Simpato."

I got up, shook hands, and made to leave. "Catch you later, Sal. Oh, can you give me a contact number for you?"

That did two things. He got my number and let Billy Peale know that he didn't have it. *Nothing to see here.*

"Chief," I said, returning the favor, "The *Quack* comes out next on Friday, right?" He nodded. "I wonder if they have Georgiana's draft of her Friday column."

Devon's eyebrows shot up. "Good thinking. Okay, stay safe out there."

"Likewise." I hadn't yet told him about the nuns, or about Ginger, or, oh god, about the man on the mountain. But at least he knew about Scooter.

"She a journalist?" Billy asked, his voice joking, his face wary.

"Nah," Devon answered for me. "Hey, Sal, that's a great idea. You wanna ask? Let me know."

Nothing a warrant wouldn't produce.

Which led me to another question, one I couldn't ask here. *What was Marigold writing about?*

CHAPTER TWELVE

It's finally Wednesday.

I realized it was both finally and only a week since I'd moved in. It felt like a lifetime, and yet the week had flown by. I hadn't thought of my defunct or dying law practice, or my definitely defunct marriage, more than perhaps four times in the past three days. The State Bar and the Family Court, both of which had been my obsession for six months, had receded in the face of the absolutely insane week I'd had.

I checked my investment account, still going strong. I did have Saul to thank for the distribution of investments. The guy was a genius with that. A crooked, unfaithful, lying, cheating scum of a genius, but okay.

I checked my email for an answer from the editor of the *Quack* to the email I'd sent last night after dragging myself home from the police station. It had been a struggle to phrase it right, and I reread it now to make sure I'd gotten the right tone.

I'm a new resident of Simpato, the daughter of the departed Keeper. Would you have time to talk to me about Simpato, especially its history of journalism? I was intrigued by the BackQuack and the gossip column, given their insights into the culture of the town. Would you be free to talk to me?

No answer yet, but it was still early. I went back to their

website. Odd, they only posted the two prior issues, not the current one or the ones from a long time ago. Surely they had archives?

I entered the newspaper's address into the map app on my computer. I couldn't walk there comfortably. Their offices were well over a mile toward Valley on the main highway. I then entered Brooks Campbell's address. It was three-quarters of a mile past the *Quack's* headquarters. If I got an answer from the editor maybe I could kill two birds with one stone. The expression brought my coffee up in my throat.

I made a quick shopping list. Another trip to the Duck Shop was in order, but at least I could walk to the grocery store this time, since I didn't need every staple ever invented. Just some food.

I sure needed to get the Prius checked. This was the second time in its life that it hadn't worked right. I would definitely need a mechanic.

It was a bit cooler today than it had been; a light jacket and a hat were definitely a good idea, given the wind. I tucked my hair under the hat and checked the look in my mirror. I still had the mirror propped against a wall. I added *ask August to hang the mirror on the wall for me* to my mental to-do list. He was a cross between a puppy and a younger brother.

I walked the four blocks to the Duck Shop. It was interesting, I thought, that everything was four blocks from my house: the police station in one direction, the Duck Shop in the opposite one, and the monastery in the third direction. Only the library and the cafe across from it were closer.

I grabbed a basket at the Duck Stop's door, since if I needed a cart I also needed the car. Cruising the aisles, I saw what I knew to be true but that hadn't been as apparent in my interactions during the past week. Almost all of the shoppers were either Latinas or tourists. Almost no Latino men, almost no nonLatinos at all, except for couples in shorts and sweatshirts with wine-related logos and caps, buying the kind of food you buy when you only have a coffee-maker in your room. Prepackaged charcuterie, baguettes, expensive cheeses, wine.

I weighed the apples I wanted, grabbed a head of lettuce, looked over the early strawberries. The more I thought of it, though, a prepackaged charcuterie plate with a baguette would make a mighty nice offering to the Campbells. I added those to the basket, then hunted down some sliced sandwich cheese, some yogurt, and another package of chicken thighs. Who knows, I might be moved to make actual dinner without burning those.

The checkout lines were all long, and any line I got into would immediately transform itself into the slowest one. It was my fate. We inched forward.

"Mrs. Keeper!" a woman said.

I looked over at the other line. It was one of the women from the group that had arrived first to the driveway last night. I smiled and waved. "Sandra, is it?"

She laughed. "No, I'm Cara. Sandra has short hair. How did it go?"

People had turned to look at us. "You're the Keeper?" "*Ahí está la Keeper.*" "Hola, Mrs. Keeper!" I felt myself blushing. "Hi," I said. So much for anonymity, ever again.

"You going to do Thursday too? That's what everyone's saying. I saw it on WAD."

I'd forgotten about the Facebook page. Of course that was where I could find all the information anyone would ever need, true or otherwise. "I'll post if I am," I said.

"Or just tell Andie," Cara said. Others in line giggled. "That girl is better than Facebook and the *Quack* put together!"

"How would I find her?" I asked. Not that I was going to have her be my megaphone, but it would be good to know in case I wanted something to get around.

"Ahem." I looked at the checker. I was now at the front of the line. And the checker was Andie. "People don't notice us as real humans," she said. "But we are."

I blushed again. She spoke truth. "Sorry. I'm just meeting so many people all at once . . ."

"No worries," she said, sliding my groceries across the scanner. "This stuff has loads of salt, you know. Makes your ankles swell. But if you're having someone over, you know, and he likes an appetizer, this is nice. And if he's in good shape, you know, from work that he has to be in good shape for . . ."

Cara giggled from the next line. "There are no secrets in Sin-Pato."

"Except the ones you keep," Andie said to me. "That's why we need a Keeper."

★ ★ ★

Cara joined me on the sidewalk. "Anyone know a good mechanic? My car's been acting up," I said. We walked back along Main Street. It was a longer way around for me, but I wanted to talk to her.

She looked at the sky. "Might rain," she said. "I thought those cars didn't break."

"They don't usually," I said. "But it's been acting funny for a few days. Wouldn't start last night." I knew now that anything I said would get around, so I was careful not to say too much.

"There used to be a good garage here in Simpato, but the old guy retired and his son had better things to do, he said, than fix beat-up old cars for folks here in town. Kind of unusual, because most kids love it here and even if they go to college elsewhere, they eventually come back. Like Scooter. He went to Santa something or other, the UC, and even though it took ten years, he came back."

I nodded, careful not to answer.

"So, a mechanic? Can your car get to Cragstown? There's a whole bunch up there. Or you can go down to Valley, plenty of everything, if you think the car will go thirty miles."

"I'm not sure it will go that far. Local, probably. Anyone closer than Cragstown?" I thought about that road up the mountain. I wouldn't want to break down there.

"I'll give it some thought," Cara said.

It wasn't until I was home and unpacking the groceries that I realized how odd that whole conversation was. Unlike every other conversation I'd had here, in which people were eager to suggest someone or other, or their cousin, or nephew for something, Cara had been less than forthcoming on the mechanic issue.

Perhaps I'd post the question on the WAD.

On the computer, I first checked my email, since the flip phone didn't give me internet access. What a habit that was, the constant contact. There was an email from the editor of the *Quack*. It was short. *I can see you anytime between ten and noon today. Please text prior to visiting. Ed.*

So, was his name Ed or was that short for Editor? I double-checked the mast. Edwina.

I was typing a quick reply to the *Quack*'s editor when I heard a tentative knock on my back door. It was too gentle for August, who would have blasted his horn upon arrival anyway. The nuns came to the front door. I peeked out and recognized Andie.

"I'm on my break," she said without preamble. If it was her ten minutes, she'd spent five of them getting here. "There's a mechanic up in Cragstown who used to live here. He works for a shop up there. I hear he's terrific with cars like yours, with the battery."

How the hell had she heard that I needed a mechanic? "Did Cara go back to the store and tell you?" I asked.

"Uh, yeah. No. She texted me."

What was this? For a town with no privacy boundaries, the

request for a mechanic was causing a lot of caginess. "Well, good, I appreciate it. Can I have his name?"

She looked a little abashed. "Um."

I waited. She'd come all the way over here on her short time off to do this.

"Call Crag-Val Garage. You can find the number online. Ask for Carlos."

"Thanks," I said.

"He's good," she added.

"Thanks," I said again.

"Okay, well I'd better get back."

I tried a smile. "Is there something I should know?"

She looked away. "Uh, he used to live in Simpato, but now he lives in Cragstown. Gotta go," she said.

Back inside I looked up Crag-Val online and found the number. They had a decent website, pretty slick for an auto shop, and photos of their mechanics grinning uncomfortably. No one was named Carlos.

Still, I called. A woman answered the phone, identifying only the shop name. I asked about an appointment for the Prius. "Sure, how about Monday next week?" I figured it was as good as I was going to get, and it gave me time to arrange for Carinna to follow me over, in case it either broke down or I had to leave it there.

"By the way, does someone named Carlos work there? He was the one recommended to me."

"Carlos? Sure. You want an appointment with him? That's gonna be a couple of weeks. He's pretty booked up."

"No, it doesn't matter. Anyone who can fix a Prius would be great."

She took my name and number—damn, I'd given her the flip phone number and by tomorrow I'd have my new old number back—and the best I could do in the way of description of the problem, and booked me for Monday at ten.

I fixed my hair and changed into a mauve sweater that flattered my complexion. I hoped the Prius would make the drive without complaint. From there, I would make a quick hop to the Campbells—my good deed for the week.

I wondered if there was Uber or Lyft in Simpato.

The Prius started right up. Before I could back out, the flip phone beeped. What an ugly little ringtone. I answered it. A man's voice said, "Mrs. DeVine?"

I acknowledged that it was me.

"This is Carl, Carlos from the garage. I was told you called for an appointment."

"I did, but I got one with someone else for Monday at ten. I heard you're booked for a couple of weeks."

"I got some room right now, if you can come up."

I was torn: the *Quack* or the Prius?

I hesitated, "I have an appointment right now . . ."

"Or tell you what," he said, mistaking my indecision for concern, "if you're worried that your car won't make it up the mountain, I can come to you. I know a Prius isn't supposed to break, but those cars can be squirrely. I'm picking up some parts down in the Duck. I can be there around one."

Wow. This place was really special. No wonder Cara and Andie didn't want to give out Carlos's name. They'd never get an appointment with him if everyone knew.

"Thank you," I gushed. That would give me three hours to drop in at the *Quack*, make my duty call to the Campbells, and be home well in time. And if the Prius gave out on me, we wouldn't be far and help would be on its way. I gave him the address. "See you at one."

"You bet," he said. "Stay safe till then."

If I could whistle, I would have, all the way to the *Quack*.

★ ★ ★

Main Street crossed the Valley River two blocks beyond the library, via a charming arched bridge with wide sidewalks on either side of the road. I realized that here was where the Brownies had "bridged" to Girl Scouts, as had been reported in The Nose the Friday before. It must have been adorable. And now the Nose was no longer.

At the stop sign I rolled down my window and could hear the river bumbling below, full of last week's rain. The thought of a man, hogtied and drowned, superimposed itself over the bucolic scene, followed swiftly by the memory of being bound in the storage unit myself. I shivered. Quickly I pressed the accelerator, but the Prius stayed motionless at the stop sign. "What?" I said to it, smacking the steering wheel. It hiccupped and jumped forward into the intersection. I slammed the brakes.

Thank goodness this man Carlos made house calls, though this car needed a therapist, not a mechanic.

I turned onto the main highway, the Prius now humming softly to itself. We followed the course of the river, the trees greening gently on the roadside, to a turnoff on the side opposite the river. A small two-story grey building with a gravel parking lot announced the name of the *Quack* on the first floor. I got out, and as I approached I could see a sign pointing up to the second floor, with a dentist and a massage therapist's office. To the side was a dingy-looking nail salon with its lights off. A full-service stop if there ever was one.

Edwina met me at the door. She stood nearly six feet tall, broad shouldered and square jawed, with frosted blonde hair cut in a smooth bob. She held out a manicured hand to shake mine. "Sal DeVine, eh?" I heard a Canadian accent beneath the purr of her voice. "The new Keeper?"

I nodded.

"Ed Sharp."

"Great name for an editor," I said, shaking her hand.

"Come in, sit down. Coffee?" She left, returning with two

cups. "Anything in it?" She had cream, sugar, and sweeteners on a tray. I took a sugar.

"So, welcome to Simpato. Land of the Duck, the No-duck, the Duckless, and of course, the *Quack*. All because some ancient white guy was too drunk to get the name right."

I grinned. I was going to like Edwina.

"But I've got very limited time, alas. So let's get down to it. What are you here for? Back issues, you can get them at the library. Ads? Our rep will reach out. Letters to the editor? Send 'em to me. Complaints about the garbage pickup, the street sweepers, the clogged street drains, or anything else about the town? Send them to the mayor. Nothing will change, but you'll feel better. If anyone can find the mayor, that is."

"Where *is* Mayor Solis?" I asked. I was still parsing through her list.

"Where? He's either dead someplace on Mount Santabella, in which case the coyotes will have a feast and the turkey vultures will lead our delicious police chief to him, or he's shacked up with—" She stopped. "What are you here for?"

Wow, I wished she'd finished that sentence.

I took a deep breath. "Ed, I need to know something. It's tricky." Though given how voluble she was, maybe I could just hint at it and she'd talk her way into answering. "I've been reading Georgiana Noyes's columns. I'm an estates lawyer, and I know about death and all. And I need to know if, you know, she had any heirs . . ." Since that was my field.

I wondered why I hadn't thought of that before. After all, *follow the money.*

"Follow the money," Ed said. I jumped. Had I said it out loud? I nodded. "I can't give out personnel records, though the police have asked for the name of whoever should be notified, and I told them she hadn't listed anyone on her forms. Did someone contact you about that?"

I shook my head. "No, it's not that. I'm just trying to find out, oh hell, look, Ed, I'm trying to find out if she knew anyone had an animus against her before she died. Sometimes it's someone who inherits. As you said, follow the money. *Qui bono? Who benefits?* But sometimes the money doesn't lead to a will or a family member. It leads to a business partner or a failed deal, or . . ."

"Ah, yes. Of course. Anatra LLC. I wonder. Now that she's gone, poor soul, I wonder who gets her interest, or however that works."

I just learned more in a sentence than I had in an hour on the internet. The name *Anatra* was familiar. I wondered who the agent was. "Do you know who the owners or managers of Anatra are?" I asked.

Ed shook her head. "I'm not completely clear on how all this works. The Montefuscos, of course, had a big part of it back in the day."

I froze. "The Montefuscos? The man who, what, died about ten years ago?"

"Yeah, him. Before my time, really. But I wonder if Georgiana still had a part in it, and who would get her, what, parts?"

"Shares. And the property. And the development potential."

"Good questions, Sal." She seemed lost in her own mind. I brought her back to earth.

"So, if Georgiana owned some property that was going to be developed, and it used to be owned by the Montefuscos, and now it wasn't going to be developed . . . and now she's dead . . ."

"And the mayor," Edwina said. "Her nemesis the mayor, now missing."

I nodded. "You're the journalist," I said. "Is there a story here?"

Edwina looked out her window, staring out over the main road to Valley. "Probably. Probably. I wonder."

I made my move. "Do you have whatever Georgiana was working on, especially for The Nose, before she died? She died on a Saturday, so you must have had her column for Monday, even though of course you didn't run it. Or at least a draft sent to you for editing. Or something for the column on Friday?"

Edwina picked up a pencil and chewed the end, her perfect lipstick marking the wood. "You know, she focused on gossip, tidbits of information about the townspeople. Who was seen at a local play, who graduated, and even something as personal as the fact that an old friend of the librarian has returned. And, of course, the new Keeper." She winked.

"Yeah, that sort of thing," I said, my heart beating faster. "Can we look at the drafts? Maybe get some ideas?"

"I'll rummage around, see what I can come up with," Ed said. "But I can't let you see them. They're proprietary, you know. I may run them; I may not. But I can't share them."

Damn. So close. "Give it some thought. I'd love to see the drafts."

"So sorry. But do go over to the library. Scooter's a wealth of information. Someone with his degree and his smarts could do better than the Simpato Library, but he's got his reasons."

It made me wonder why Edwina Sharp was at the *Quack*. I guess she had her reasons too.

"It was good to meet you." She stood up. Interview over.

We shook hands; I saw myself out. I was halfway to the Campbells when the import of what she'd said hit me. I pulled over and texted her. *You should send the drafts to the police. I think they might be important.*

Not without a warrant, she answered immediately. *Long live freedom of the press.*

CHAPTER THIRTEEN

The Campbells lived in a single-story redwood home, with a gracious side-deck that opened onto a terraced garden. The earth had been turned over but planting hadn't begun. At the end of the garden, several rows of vines stood waiting for Spring's signal to bud. The sun shone off the droplets of water clinging to potted geraniums that formed the railing at the deck's edge, and trailing nasturtiums wandered down to the garden below.

I parked in their circular driveway, and the front door opened before I could walk up the ramp to the porch. Framed by the doorway was a tall, thin man with a shock of white hair that stood nearly straight up. His long face was reddened from age and weather, and as I approached he smiled a wide, white-toothed grin that crinkled his blue eyes. "Oh, little Sal! My goodness, a grown-up woman! Catherine," he shouted, turning away, "come and say hello to Sal!"

He pulled me in and wrapped me in his long-armed hug. "My oh my. You look just like your mother. So very good to see you."

A whirring sound brought Catherine, seated in an electric wheelchair. "There you are," she said, her voice barely above a whisper, contrasting with Brooks's bellow. "Welcome, my dear. Let her in, Brooks," she added. "Don't keep her on the doorstep all morning." She gave me a conspiratorial little smile, then turned her chair around and rolled into the house.

"Right, right," Brooks said. "And what have you here?"

I felt a little abashed at the supermarket baguette and charcuterie in plastic wrap, and at my smug stereotyping that suggested these as a generous offering, but I handed the bag over. "Excellent," Brooks said. "Catherine, she's brought some cold cuts and bread for us. We can add that to our platter."

He strode ahead of me and past Catherine, who was rolling onto the deck I'd seen from the driveway. An open-plan kitchen with an island and gleaming counters separated the living area from the rest of the house, and on one of those counters sat a black tray with several cheeses, crackers, and olives, next to a small plate with cookies. All store-bought, but all high-end. China coffee cups stood waiting by a copper espresso-cappuccino machine.

Catherine turned to me. "I don't cook anymore. Sixty years was plenty, and besides, I can only stand for about five minutes before my leg gives way. Brooks here is always threatening to go to cooking school and take over meals, but for now the deli in Valley delivers. Coffee or espresso?"

I watched as Brooks expertly handled our choices, then I took my foaming cappuccino to the deck. He pulled out a little folding table for Catherine and placed the snacks within reach. He and I took well-cushioned chairs, he under the umbrella, me out in the gentle sun. "I don't want to give my dermatologist any more work than I already do," he said as he chose the shade. "I've already funded her children's education and probably a boat or two with my Scotch-Irish complexion. We weren't meant to live in sunny California," he smiled.

"So," I said brightly, "how wonderful to find out you're in Simpato."

"Yes, indeed, the perfect place to retire. Cooler than Sacramento, warmer than San Francisco, and all the wine you could drink. Of course, to get to a decent doctor we go all the way to

Davis," he said, mentioning the world-renowned medical center at the university, "but as long as I'm driving it's a small price to pay. And how are you settling in?"

"The ghosts not too present?" Catherine added softly.

I took a sip of the excellent cappuccino. Brooks's voice sounded so much like my dad's. For the first time in a decade, I felt sheltered, safe. My hands started to shake. I wanted to curl up in Brooks' fatherly embrace, to lean my cheek against Catherine's soft, lightly lined one.

Brooks leaned forward. "Sal, what's troubling you? Tell us everything."

"Nothing," I said. "It's just that in the week I've been here I've been on the roller-coaster ride from hell, and I don't know what's going on." I sounded fourteen. This wouldn't do. I needed to pull it together. They were probably the only people on earth who knew my parents well, and yet knew Simpato too.

I took a deep breath. "Brooks, Catherine," it still felt funny calling them by their first names, "you're on the WAD site. What was my mother doing with this Keeper business?"

Brooks looked out over his tiny vineyard. "Oh, not too much. Just a little coffee klatch now and—"

"Oh, knock it off, Brooks. She's serious. Sal, your mother was a very special person. The hole in our hearts will never close, losing her and your dad. But she was something else. Ethereal. A visionary. And every week, all summer long, and in the two years after she moved to Simpato year-round she even held sessions in the winter, she would hold her heart open for anyone with a secret. They could come and tell her, and she would keep their secrets safe. It was something no one had done before, and no one since. She called it her *mitzvah*. And I'm afraid that's what drove them away."

"Nonsense," Brooks interrupted. "Stan had fantasized about sailing to Hawai'i since I'd known him. They just finally up and went, that's all. Bad timing, storms. Nothing at all to do with that Keeper business."

"Did they tell you they were leaving?" I asked. "They didn't tell me, or Dahlia."

"No," Brooks said.

"Not in so many words," Catherine said softly. I looked to her for more. Her pale cheeks colored a bit. "Alta called me," Catherine continued, her eyes on me. "She said she was going to have to break her Keeper promise for the first time ever, and she was despondent over it. But she said an innocent man's freedom was at stake. She drove over here and we sat on this very deck. She told me, well, she told me that a young man had come to her with a devastating secret about, well, the only murder in Simpato in ages. He'd told her about what led up to the killing, and it was clear that he hadn't done it. With what he had confided, Alta knew who had.

"But the young man in question was arrested for murder. No one believed he would do something like that, but he couldn't explain what happened; he was not the brightest fellow, especially since he refused to name his friend. His friend, who'd murdered his abusive, horrible father. And Alta knew."

I felt my heart stop. I thought back to what August had said. He knew who had murdered the real estate agent. But he never said it was the agent's son. And Scooter, August, and the third boy, the young Montefusco, used to hang out on Mount Santabella together. Until they didn't.

"We talked for hours," Catherine was saying. "We decided that she would go to the police, but that she would end her Keeper practice after that. It was too dangerous. The young man who'd killed his father was sent away to live with relatives, and only Alta and I, and her confidant, knew he'd done it. Alta was beside herself. She couldn't go to the police about the real murderer, and yet she was sure he'd done it. Killing is never justified, but the father mistreated the son—again, all according to your mother. And then she got a letter. She showed it to me. It was not artful, but it was clear. If she told anyone, she was next.

"We decided that she and Stan would take a little vacation, a sailing trip, nothing major, nothing like the Hawai'i trip they ended up going on, just to let things die down. And so, I guess, Stan talked her into the big sail. *That* part I never knew."

"And he was so careful, so meticulous, I knew he would be okay wherever he went," Brooks added.

I couldn't breathe.

"He registered the trip with the Coast Guard, evidently. But no one else," Brooks added. "And no one heard from them again."

I wiped the tears that were running down my face. "Excuse me," I muttered, getting up.

"Second door past the kitchen," Catherine said. "Take your time."

"You shouldn't have upset her so," I heard Brooks chiding her as I made my shaky way out of the room.

"You're the one who never knows how to guard your tongue!" she snapped back.

I ran the water in the sink just to give myself time to recover. The threatening letter was new information for me, but the rest was all things that at some level I already knew. I just hadn't thought the entire story through chronologically. And I hadn't taken in that the murderer had been the victim's son. What had Catherine said? The father was horribly abusive. How did August, my mother, and Catherine all know this—but the police didn't?

August's words came back to me: *I know who did it. But that's not the secret, because your mom knew too. It's just that he's back.*

"Who's back?" I wanted to scream. The drama that had

engulfed me this past week had been going on a long time. It seems this story was only new to me.

When I returned to the deck Brooks had angled the umbrella so it shaded more of the little table, and Catherine had wheeled herself further under its protection. I was grateful for my mother's complexion, its warmth allowing me to enjoy early Spring sunshine without burning.

"Let's talk about more pleasant things," Catherine said. "Though *tell me about your divorce* isn't really a jolly topic, now is it?"

I smiled. "No, not really, but I'm not devastated, either."

"I'm glad to hear it," Brooks said. "I assume a decent settlement?"

"Absolutely."

"Are you going to set up your practice here in Simpato, or down in Valley?" he asked.

Now there was another unfortunate topic, one I didn't want to broach. "I think I'm going to give myself a few months to get my bearings, recover a bit," I replied.

"A good settlement indeed, then," he winked.

"Indeed." I looked at my watch. I'd been there less than a half an hour, but it felt like a lifetime. "Maybe you could tell me why you moved here," I suggested.

"The usual reasons," Catherine said. "Nothing that would interest a young person."

"Another topic for another day, then," I said. "Brooks, can I ask you a legal question?" That would get him off and running, I was sure, and I realized I had a gold-mine resource here.

"Certainly, my dear. Fire away. Though I've not been keeping up quite as I ought, you know. I should take a look at the State Bar site," I felt my stomach drop, "see what the newest continuing education requirements are, so I can stay current."

Oh, don't do that! "Well, I'm sure you're well-versed enough to give me an overview. I've been considering forming an LLC for my practice, when I do start back up again. Can you refresh me on everything an LLC does or can be?"

"I would certainly encourage you to set yourself up properly, Sal. As I know you know, companies can take a few forms. You would probably choose to be a PC."

"Politically correct to the end," Catherine said. I gave the obligatory smile, though I knew that he was referring to a professional corporation.

"But an LLC is a form of company that has a managing member, who is the front-man, if you will—"

"Front-woman, front-person," Catherine said.

Brooks spoke over her. "—who is the face of the company. There are other investors, who have a membership interest, like investors or stockholders, but they're just called members. They all work under an operating agreement that defines what business they do, how the interests are held, whether they can sell them—"

"Or inherit them?" I asked.

"Naturally, that would be of interest to you as an estates lawyer. That would depend on the operating agreement. If it said you could sell your membership interest, or leave it to someone, or whether it all passed to the other members if you died—"

"Heaven forbid," Catherine said.

"The inheritance or sales, all that would be defined by the operating agreement. And if you could sell, the new member would have to be eighteen at least, unless an adult took ownership on their behalf, and whether or not they could vote, I mean in the company, not in an election . . ."

"So, if, say, there were an LLC that owned a piece of property. And the member of the LLC, who had the majority membership died, his interest could go to the other members, or to his estate, depending on what the operating agreement said?"

"That's right."

"And if, wait a minute! If the shares went to someone who wasn't eighteen . . ."

"They'd be held in trust, most likely, until she was of age."

"Or he," I said, thinking aloud.

"I was just trying to be modern," Brooks said.

But I wasn't listening. I was thinking about Anatra, LLC, that used to be Montefusco, LLC. That owned the land that was going to be developed, until it wasn't. And Georgiana Noyes was the managing member of Anatra.

I looked at Brooks and Catherine, enjoying the sunshine, taking an interest in me. My parents should be here with them, having coffee. But they're gone because someone threatened my mother.

"I really appreciate your time and loved talking with you. As soon as I'm settled, let's do this again." I stood up quickly. I needed to hurry home and look up a few things. And the mechanic was coming in less than two hours.

"We'd love that. You make us feel alive again," Catherine said. "It's been so quiet the past few years. Do come again."

I bent down and kissed her soft cheek. "Thank you. I will." I turned to Brooks. "And thank you for the law lesson. You filled in a major blank."

"Maybe we can talk shop again soon," Brooks said. "You may look like your mother, but you think like Stan. Be careful pulling out of the drive. The drivers around here are outrageous."

CHAPTER FOURTEEN

I had enough time to drive home and do a little research before the mechanic was due. I pulled in, the Prius purring like a kitten—isn't it always that way, I thought, the tooth stops hurting the moment you walk into the dentist's office—and saw a note flapping on my back door.

Your phone doesn't answer. Ginger called, need to talk asap. Sister Marigold.

I read it again. She would have my old number, but where would she have gotten it? Maybe Sassafras or Sorghum? It was testament to the fact that I'd acclimatized to Simpato to such an extent that I barely chuckled at the names.

No, she must have gotten it from Carinna.

Not for the first time, I wondered what Margo Schwartz was writing about. I checked my watch. I didn't have time, only half an hour until the mechanic was due. I didn't know how punctual he would or wouldn't be.

Unlike Marigold, I didn't have a way to get her personal cell— did nuns have personal cell phone numbers? They weren't *chastity and poverty* nuns, so she probably did. But I didn't have it.

What I did have was the mechanic's cell phone info.

I texted the number he'd called on. *I need to run a quick errand. I'll be back in an hour. Okay?*

I immediately got a thumbs-up. Whew. Looked like Carlos was flexible as well as convenient. He was going to get a five-star review from me on Yelp—or was it a five-Duck review?

I switched on the computer and immediately went to the Secretary of State webpage. I was right. Montefusco LLC had become Anatra about ten years ago. I could see Georgiana's name listed as an owner on an updated statement of information, and I also noted that she had inserted herself as Agent not too long ago, probably when she felt it was safe to show her connection. I wished I could see who any other members were.

I opened Google Maps and got the coordinates for the vineyard property, then ran a search on that. I couldn't even be surprised to learn that it was owned by Anatra LLC. Of course it was. The big question was, *who gets her membership interest now that she's gone?* Operating agreements weren't filed anywhere public.

I looked at the time. I had to get over to the monastery. A young girl with nothing to do with all of this sordid business was probably in danger. Poor Ginger, with her family back in Fresno, judging her and yet waiting for that baby she just hadn't been ready to have.

I locked up again and went out the front, checking to see if anything else had been left for me. I was surprised that Marigold had left the note on the back door, since the nuns seemed to come to the front, but maybe she didn't want to be seen. I walked the few blocks to the monastery.

Should I go right up to the front or walk around the back? The front door was closed, and I didn't try it to see if it was locked. I just went through the little side gate and around to the back.

"Good choice," I heard Marigold's voice before I saw her. She was standing by the chain-link fence that abutted the playground, partially concealed by the shrubs along the edge. "I could see you coming down the sidewalk from here, so I could intercept you if you tried the oak doors. Come," she added, gesturing to the door in the side of the building.

We once again cut through that amazing kitchen. Another door was propped open, and I could see a hot tub and the frosted doors of what looked like a steam room. Pretty posh for a convent.

She led me into the corridor with the individual rooms. We passed hers, though, and quickly stepped into another room. This one had remnants of an occupant who favored pastels and little stuffed kitties. Clean and neat, as I'm sure all the rooms were, but this room exuded *teen-aged girl.*

"Ginger's room?" I asked. Marigold nodded. "She left these things?"

"Yeah. I cleaned the room—Mother Sassafras's orders—but she left the kittens and a little blanket she'd been crocheting for the baby before she, er, lost it."

I felt the girl's conflicted grief. I shoved that thought aside.

"So what did she say in that urgent call?" I asked. "I have a mechanic coming shortly, so I can't stay long."

Marigold took a folded note from her habit's skirt. "I took notes on the call, journalist's habit," she said. I laughed. "What?"

"Habit. Nun's habit, journalist's habit. Not sure you're either of those. But what did she say?"

Marigold's eyebrows stayed up as she smirked. With the wimple and her glasses she had a very nunnish look. "So, we know I'm not a real nun. But you don't believe I'm a journalist either. Okay. What do you think I'm doing here?"

I put on my lawyer-voice. "I have no idea. I'm not sure I even care. But if Ginger's in danger, you, or you and I, need to let the police know. What did she say?"

Marigold shrugged. "Have it your way. She said Scooter drove her to Santabella, the town, not the mountain, and she caught the bus to Valley. She's okay, but she's scared. Last Friday, after she and Scooter had had a little fun, Scooter told her that this was her big chance. He told her that after the service on Saturday, when she was serving the refreshments— since as a novice that was one of her main jobs—she was to tell Ephedra that she'd like to serve Georgiana personally. Ephedra usually sets up the glasses and the cookies. Nasty woman, but she's an amazing baker."

"The call . . . ?"

"Right. Because the Nose was the celebrity of the town, Scooter said she could help Ginger get away, or get modeling jobs, or something so she wouldn't have to go back to Fresno. She told him she felt too shy to do it, so he said that on Saturday he would leave the service early and help her get the glasses from Ephedra. When she came out, because the nuns leave first, he handed her a glass and told her to give it to Noyes as she walked out. Kind of as an icebreaker, so she'd be able to introduce herself and get to talking. When Ephedra saw her, she handed Ginger another glass. *Don't make a spectacle of yourself, girl,* she said. *Give this one to Salvia.*

"Somehow, I derailed this by asking to talk to you. Unfortunately, you took off without enjoying the refreshments. Georgiana thanked her, drank a few sips of lemonade, and put the glass down. Then she left."

"Do you think there was something in the lemonade?"

"In those glasses, yeah."

"Mine too."

Marigold nodded.

I felt sick. "I'm glad I didn't drink whatever was in it," I said quietly. "Too bad Ginger didn't tell the cops. They could have found the glasses, tested them."

Marigold smiled. "But that's what Ginger wanted to tell me. Because I cleaned her room, and I found the glasses in the bottom of her wardrobe."

She opened the plain wood armoire. Hanging from the rod was a single green habit, with the coif and wimple on the little shelf above the rod. At the bottom were two glasses, etched with poppies, dead ringers for mine. "Oh my god, Marigold. The police need to have those. And you need to tell them what Ginger told you!"

She shook her head. "Journalist privilege. I don't have to tell them anything. But now you do."

I looked at her. I still couldn't figure out what she was playing at. She'd just, basically, fingered Scooter as Georgiana's murderer, with Ephedra as a coconspirator, and maybe Ginger as an accidental accomplice. Whether Marigold meant to implicate Ginger or not, she definitely intended to spotlight Scooter and Ephedra. And she wanted me, who hadn't heard any of this firsthand, to go to the cops.

I certainly planned to.

"Wrap them in something," I said.

Marigold took the wimple from the shelf. Using the cloth to pick up the glasses, she wrapped them carefully and handed them to me.

"Don't screw Ginger over," she said. I looked at her but didn't answer. "Or at least don't destroy the whole monastery."

I stood up. "I'll do what I can." I took the bundle. "Did she tell you why she just so happened to save these particular glasses?"

Marigold's look got hard. "No, she didn't. And I didn't ask."

Some journalist.

"I'll see you out," Marigold said. "We'll use a different door."

We left the room and turned in the opposite direction of the kitchen. "This way."

Something was totally off-kilter here. Was Marigold dangerous or crazy? I needed to bring all this, everything I knew, to Devon. This wasn't just about some dumb property development. It was about murder—one, possibly two. Or maybe even three if the mayor was dead, and luckily not *four,* as in *mine.* At least not yet.

Should I follow her or just break for it? She was younger and, habit notwithstanding, probably faster. I followed.

We turned into the monastery's laundry room, complete with two washers, three dryers, and an ironing board. Next to a dryer-vent outlet was a narrow door, held closed by a simple hook-and-eye.

"High security," I said. My voice was even, but my heart was pounding.

She nodded. She grabbed an empty Duck Shop paper bag, and I shoved the glasses into it. "All the security they need," she said as she opened the door, letting me out near the sidewalk on the far side of the building. "There's no crime in Simpato."

CHAPTER FIFTEEN

I let myself in the front door and checked my little flip phone. No calls or messages, so I slipped off my jacket and walked to the back to hang it up. And screamed.

There in my kitchen, on a little chair, Scooter sat, reading a book. "Hey," he said.

"What the hell are you doing here?"

"Obviously reading," he said. He held up the book, *Sea Chanties of Nantucket*. "Your interests are eclectic." I glanced out the back window. Maybe the mechanic would show up and Scooter would take off. But instead he stood, put the book carefully on the counter, and grabbed me by the arm. "Come, we're going to have a chat."

I was still carrying the bag with the glasses. "I need to put this away," I said. "It's ice cream." I opened the freezer and shoved the glasses, wimple, and bag in at once.

"You should take it out of the bag or it will melt and refreeze."

I didn't dare. "No, it's good that way," I said quickly. "I don't have a lot of food in there, as you can see, so it's good to take up room."

I definitely couldn't let him see the glasses.

"Come on," he said. He pulled me forward, toward the living room.

I thought we were going out the front door, but he pulled

me into the bedroom instead. "Sit down," he said, pushing me onto the bed. His voice hissed as always, but there was plenty of menace. I started to get up again, and he pushed me harder this time. "I don't want to tie you to the bed," he said.

I was still. This couldn't be happening.

"Oh, don't worry. I'm not going to hurt you. I just want you to sit still for a minute. I'm going to tell you a bedtime story."

Scooter had lost his mind.

His eyes glittered, and his breath was quick. I sat very still.

"Once upon a time," he started, pacing a bit. I listened for the sound of the mechanic arriving. If he was punctual, he should be here in less than ten minutes. If he was late—he could be too late. "Once upon a time," he started again, "ten years ago, when I was in high school, remember?" He looked like he wanted an answer. I nodded. That seemed to suffice.

"There were three guys. I told you this part of the story already," he added, sounding normal, if squeaky, and not manic. "So, there was me, and there was August, who's slow, but he's a strong mother, and there was Carl. Like I told you, Carl was the golden boy. Me, I was me. Kids don't know how they are. Girls loved me; I was state-ranked in the four-forty."

I didn't know what a four-forty was. Should I ask?

My face seemed to have done the work for me.

"It's a track race."

He ran like a deer, down the mountain. I had forgotten to tell Devon about that.

"You were a runner?" I said, trying to delay until the mechanic arrived.

"Still am. Now I run the mountain trails. All relevant to my story. Don't jump ahead."

"Sorry," I muttered.

"I also sang in the choir, and I was in the pageant. Now, I can barely talk." His eyes glittered again. "But I can still run. Where was I? Oh, yeah. So the three amigos, we used to hang out and drink on the mountain, smoke some weed, every guy does, but we were tops. We were the kings of the class. Not August, he was like the king's bodyguard or something. He hung with me and Carl, but we were the kings. And there were the nuns."

"The nuns? You mean the Little Sisters of the Earth?"

"Yep. The old Catholic nuns had left when we were in middle school, and the new group came. Lezzies, mostly," I winced at the word but he just plowed right on, "we just felt that, and they were not real nuns because they weren't Catholic. Almost everyone in Sin-Pato belongs to Saint Francis. Except your family, right?"

"The nuns—"

"Don't rush me!" He took a deep breath. "Yeah, they were all about the earth. And they had those hilarious names. Some of them were young, and if you looked beyond the nun-habits, they were hot. Believe me, any guy can look beyond the clothes. It's an instinct. Even you look pretty hot beyond your clothes."

Great.

"And there were a couple of them that were really, really hot. You know where their kitchen is now?" I nodded. "Used to be their shower room. And all that patio up to the playground? Used to be woods."

Where Carinna and her boyfriend used to tryst, two decades before these boys had even reached puberty.

"We used to go, the three of us, and hang out in those woods and get a glimpse of the nuns showering, getting ready for bed. And since they weren't real nuns, sometimes they'd shower together. Bonanza!"

"You used to peep at nuns?"

"Not real nuns, remember? And they should have put up better curtains. Anyway, next to the shower room they had a hot tub."

Like he said, not real nuns. "They still do," I said.

"Now we're getting to the good stuff," he said.

Where was that damned mechanic? "You don't have to tell me this," I said.

"Oh, but I do. You need to understand what you're poking your nose into. So one night, Carl gets the idea that he's going to sneak into the monastery and get into that hot tub. He bet me ten bucks that he could get in there with them. August and I went along as witnesses. We hid in the bushes, and he sneaks up to the window where the showers and the hot tub are. He takes out his dick and rubs it a little, and we're all trying not to laugh. Then we look over at the hot-tub area, and one of the windows is open. Just like your window. Which is how I got in here just now. Everyone leaves their windows open here."

Right, because there's no crime in Simpato.

"Carl says, *I'm gonna get some real duck action,* and he slips into the monastery. He was a hell of an athlete. He actually gets into the room with the hot tub, the curtains are closed, but the window is open, and suddenly we hear a bunch of yelling, and the little side door bangs open. And Carl is being thrown out, pants around his ankles, and there's his dad, Mr. Montefusco, and Sebastian Solis, the future mayor, both stark naked with towels falling off them, coming after Carl."

My jaw could have hit the bed, my mouth was hanging so open.

"Yeah, amazing, right? And the towels fall off, and these two naked men grab ahold of Carl, who really can't run unless he gets his pants back up, so he's trying to yank up his jeans. At first I'm just dying laughing, but then his dad starts to beat the shit out of Carl. I mean really taking it to him. Mostly his dad; the mayor was kind of trying to pull Mr. Montefusco off of Carl, but not really trying that hard. And there was nothing August or I could do. At least that's what we thought, right?"

He actually waited for an answer. I validated. "Of course you couldn't do anything. You were kids. You'd have been crazy to jump into that."

He nodded. "I mean, Carl was strong as shit, but he was stuck because his pants were around his ankles, right? That wouldn't let him really get back on his feet, and defend himself. But the worst thing was Mr. Montefusco was just laughing at Carl. *Got your little weenie out and everything,* he said. He was taunting him and smacking him, and Solis wasn't really trying to stop it. Finally Mr. Montefusco said, *Don't bother coming home, little boy,* and went back in."

Scooter was flushed, I could see the wildness in his eyes. I didn't know what to say, so I put my hand out to touch his arm.

"Yeah, it was bad," he said, his breathing slowing.

"Didn't the nuns come out?"

He shook his head. "Not real nuns, that's for sure.

"I guess they got dressed and left; we didn't stick around. We got Carl and took him to August's house. We couldn't go to mine because we lived over in the mobile-home park; everyone would have known. But August's mom was really cool, in an old-fashioned Mexican way. His dad was a trucker, drove long hauls, so he wasn't there a lot, but he was a pretty good guy too, from what we knew. But it was just August and his mom, most of the time. Anyway, she took care of Carl.

"Carl didn't come back to school. He stayed at August's for a few days. Then Mr. Montefusco was found dead in the river."

Scooter was finally quiet, his rasping, whispery voice was stilled. We sat on my bed, for the moment not adversaries, as the tiles clicked into place in my head. Scooter was staring out the window of my bedroom toward the street. He looked so young. Though he had to be twenty-eight, he seemed, for now, like the very scared teen he had to have been.

"The cops interviewed us all. I told most of the truth, that we were all out drinking and had gone by the monastery, and there'd been the scene with Solis and Montefusco, but I was at a track meet overnight—county championships—the night that Mr. Montefusco was killed. August tried to lie to the cops, I guess, but you know how he is, and they arrested him. Mr. Future Mayor never said a word. A scandal like that would have ended any political aspirations he had. No one told. But your mom did."

I startled. I had been lulled into Scooter's *bedtime story.* "What did my mom have to do with it?"

"No one really knows, but word was she went to the cops, told them something she knew as Keeper, and August was freed."

"What happened to Carl?"

Scooter's face was hard again, the arrogant surfer-dude. "He was sent to live with an aunt in LA or something. Never was arrested. Never came back to school."

"You and August graduated?"

"Yep. August went to work at the same trucking company as his dad. Still works there, loading trucks. I went to UC Santa Barbara."

"Do you know why my parents left?" Here at last was a chance to ask that question. "Was it right after my mother talked to the cops?"

"Hell if I know. I was eighteen, I was thinking about graduation. All I know is—well, yeah, it was after—after they let August out. And your folks left that March, I heard they were going on a sailing trip, and they never came back. I'm sorry for your loss."

The sentiment clunked in light of the story, but I didn't want to challenge him. "Thanks for telling me all this, Scooter," I said, sliding off the bed. "I've got a mechanic coming—he should be here by now—to check out the Prius. It's been acting weird."

Scooter was in his normal phase again and let me out of the bedroom. "Nice. Who knew mechanics made—wait. Who's this mechanic?"

"Don't know. His name is Carlos. Coming down from Cragstown."

Scooter's eyes glittered again. "Are you fucking kidding me?" His voice screeched higher. "Are you insane?"

No, but you are.

"I'm going to wait right here. Make sure he doesn't do something he'll regret."

"What are you talking about?"

"You're an idiot," he said, striding to the back door. "Tell you what. Let's see what this Carlos looks like. If he's Mexican, I leave. If he's a good-looking white motherfucker with green eyes, you're going straight to the cops."

"Kind of a reverse racist thing?" I said before I could stop myself.

He chuckled. "No, you dumb bitch. You know I went to college, right? Everything was great. Learned to surf, I was free of this stupid place with its duck jokes and its past, until I ran into my old buddy Carl. As soon as he resurfaced, I started having nightmares again, like I did my whole last semester of high school.

"Carl needed money. I liked to look stuff up, so I helped him figure out how to get his money from his inheritance. And Carl, he had something to help me get by. Carl got me hooked on meth in Santa Barbara. I couldn't take the nightmares. And he was dealing, big time. And he was the only one who'd understand, and he couldn't tell anyone, either. Because I knew he'd killed his dad, and he knew I was there that night he got his ass whupped. I wasn't the only one who played that scene over and over in his head. But I also wasn't the one who got beat up in front of my friends, half-naked with my pants around my ankles. In front of my friends," he repeated, "who didn't help me."

I reached for his hand, but he pulled away, deep in his story. "One night a couple of years ago, on the beach, we were all high as kites, there was a big fight with another bunch of guys. One of them called Carl a weenie. That set him off. Carl pulled a knife, and I was kind of backing out of the fight, but he yelled at me, *you gonna stand and watch again?* I would have tried to help, but I'm not a fighter, I'm a runner, and Carl turned on me. He swung his knife and cut my throat. He went to jail; I got clean."

My god. "Still clean?"

"Mostly. I use cannabis to regulate the flashbacks and keep me down. But it spurts back up. I know what this shit can do to you, even in small doses." He smiled, and handsome as he was, that smile was plain ugly. "Even just a little bit, to a lady who isn't used to using."

I thought of Georgiana, and Ginger helping, maybe even Ephedra. And my almost becoming a part of the equation, except that I really didn't care for lemonade. And the glasses in my freezer. I needed to call Devon, now.

But Scooter couldn't stop talking. "I came home a year ago, started doing the library thing. I had my degree in library science. I always liked to put things in order, look stuff up. But it's hard to get a job if you're an ex-addict, and I needed a safe place to regroup. I was getting it together, when Solis, the mayor, kind of roped me into the development thing. He was opposing the development of the vineyard property, because it was Carl's and Georgiana's property, and he never forgave Carl for crashing in on him at the convent. Carl inherited the land from his dad."

"But it was in something called an LLC," I said.

"So you know this already?"

"A little. But not what Georgiana had to do with it." Nothing I was going to tell Scooter, anyway.

"Georgiana bought into Mr. Montefusco's LLC, right after she moved up here from Valley. She'd been on some sort of board and gotten into trouble, so I guess she figured she'd try her luck in a smaller town. She started writing for the *Quack* and helping Mr. Montefusco manage the land. Since Carl doesn't know a damn thing about—wait. What's that sound?"

I heard it too. It was a car at the back of my house, pulling up into my driveway behind the Prius. "Hopefully, the mechanic," I said.

"Be careful what you wish for." Scooter looked out the kitchen window. "It's that motherfucker. He's here. Come on," he said, pulling me by the arm away from the window, toward the front door.

"I'm calling the police," I said.

"You're coming with me," he replied, an iron grip on my arm. He twisted it up behind my back, and pain shot through my shoulder. I bent forward as he dragged me down the walk. If I screamed, the mechanic would come. I tried, and felt a plastic bag shoved into my mouth. "Shut up, don't bite down, just come along nicely," he hissed. "If you bite the bag, some very ugly stuff will get into your system." He jerked my arm up higher, and I had to force myself not to struggle.

His truck was parked out front, and he opened the door, very gentlemanly, helped me up into the cab, then shoved me into the seat. He wrapped the shoulder harness around my neck before buckling it in to the seat-belt latch. I was bent forward in a strange and awkward position.

As soon as he let go of my arm I pulled the bag out of my mouth and threw it on the floor.

He was fast. He was around the front and into the driver's side before I could untangle the seat belt and jump out. I heard a click. "These new trucks have safety latches, so your kids can't jump out," he said as I tried the door.

I knew there was a lock release on my side, there had to be for exit safety, but as I fumbled for the catch on the seat belt we took off so fast it threw me against the dash. Hard. "Sit back. You know I'm not going to hurt you, or I would have there in your house."

"Where are we going?" I said. I pulled the belt off from my neck and sat up.

"To the mountain. To the place where Georgiana died. Look, if you don't stop it now—" I was fully out of the seat belt finally—"I'm going to have to do something. Like make you swallow that whole bag." I sat still.

He took the back route, more deserted, and parked up in a vineyard. I hoped that would attract attention. Maybe Tilly was driving around and would see the truck and tell Devon.

"Why?" I asked, hoping to keep him talking.

"I need to show you something. And I need to get you away from Carl."

He opened my door. "I got to do this," he rasped, pulling my hands behind my back. He knotted something around them, so tight I felt the circulation in my hands stop. "Nice veins," he said. I froze.

He yanked my head back again, and shoved the plastic baggie in deep. I gagged against it, but it was in too far to spit out. "Come on, get moving."

He started up the path. "I'm going to put you on a leash if you don't walk faster," he said. I sped up, stumbled on a small rock, and without my hands to steady myself, I lurched into him. "Okay, we'll go a little slower. But not too slow."

"Why are you doing this?" I tried to asked again. It was garbled, but he got it.

"Like I just said, you're not stupid. I'm going to hide you in a cave, just like I was going to do with Georgiana. To protect you."

I kept pushing the bag with my throat and it shifted toward my teeth. I gargled. "Okay, I'll take it out," he said, "but I'm warning you. Anything, and I mean *anything*, and I'm going to pour the whole thing down your throat. Got it?" I nodded. "Open up."

I opened my lips and he reached for the bag. Then stopped, his eyes glittering. "Oh, this is so tempting," he said, looking down at me. He licked his lips. Was it tempting to use the contents, I wondered, or force me to? "If you were a little younger . . ." He took the bag out, and put it in his jeans pocket. I breathed a trembling sigh. "Be good now," he said. I nodded. He grabbed my arm again, and once again we started walking.

"Why did you want to hide Georgiana?" I asked finally. My throat was dry, my voice a caricature of Scooter's.

"I was just going to scare her into making some sensible moves. Because as we both know, Carl is back. She was going to put that in her column. And the whole thing was going to come out. The murder, the drugs, the fact that I was a witness, all of it. I wanted to give her a little something to think about."

"So you got Ginger to drug her lemonade," I said.

He stopped. He turned to me. His eyes narrowed. "How did you know about that?" Oh, no. If I told him, Marigold would be in danger. "After all I did for that little bitch, she told you?"

I shook my head. "No, I just figured it out. But I thought you were clean?"

He laughed. "You can get any kind of drug up in Cragstown. Where do you think I got this?" He held up the little baggie. "And now that Carl's out of jail, he's ready to supply anyone. So I picked up a little from him, and someone gave that dumb kid Ginger some to put in Georgiana's glass."

Someone?

"I still don't get why."

"You are slow, for a lawyer. Georgiana knew that Carl was back. Hell, they're partners, except that instead of ninety-five percent to Carl, five percent to the Nose, it was now the other way around. I don't think Carl knew that when he came back north. But he found out, because each time we contacted this Anatra to get some money for him, I had to sign something that gave Anatra a certain percentage of Carl's share in exchange for, like, a couple of grand. He didn't know that he was giving up pieces of the vineyard for, well, peanuts.

"Solis knew that the Pathways development had just been approved in Cragstown, because he's boyfriends with the mayor there. Georgiana had been pimping her development in Simpato and didn't know that the development wasn't going to be her little parcel. That's the surprise that Solis was going to announce at the monastery.

"Solis and I had argued about telling the cops Carl was back. I didn't want Georgiana to put the word out in her column that Monday, which she would have done the minute she found out she wasn't going to get the development. I wanted her out of the monastery before the announcement, and I wanted to give her just a little scare. Give her some drugs, take her up the mountain, hide her in a cave. I know every inch of this mountain. Solis didn't like it, but I knew that was the best way. And he'd stay clean, *uninvolved,* because he wasn't in good enough shape to go up the mountain. But you know what Solis was most worried about?"

"What?"

"You."

"Me?"

"When he heard that the Keeper's daughter was here, he was petrified. What if your mom told you what she knew? Whatever it was that set August free? Like the fact that he'd let Montefusco beat up and humiliate his son. That he'd been playing around in the hot tub at the monastery, though given how he swings, maybe it was with Montefusco himself. He sure wouldn't be mayor anymore.

"Not because he was gay, well, not only because, but his

involvement in the Montefusco thing would do in his mayorship. And without him, the Council could change its mind and approve the Nose's development. It was a lot fancier than whatever will go up in Cragstown. Pathways would jump at the switch in a flash. And Solis would be the laughing stock of the Duck. I just laughed at him. I knew how to make sure you didn't talk."

I shivered. Now he was going to make sure of that. I had to get away. "So you were going to drug my lemonade too?"

"Nah, that was Ephedra's idea. She wanted to make you look like a lunatic, just in case you got in the way. Who knows, maybe she was one of the nuns in the tub with Montefusco that night. With their nun-suits and me being a kid, I wouldn't know. But mostly, she's a pretty big investor in the Pathways project up at Cragstown. Pretty funny for an eco-nun, huh? But I told Solis he didn't have to worry about you."

I didn't say anything.

"Don't you want to know why?"

I still didn't answer.

"Because you've got a little secret too. At the service, that's what I was showing Solis. The State Bar site. Little Miss Fraud, herself. Wouldn't that look great in Georgiana's column? Too bad she never got to put it in. But that wasn't my fault."

"You're still guilty," came a voice behind us—a voice I knew. The voice from the storage unit. "Let's see. Kidnapping, hiding information from the cops, assault, what else?"

Scooter whirled around. "Carl. What the hell are you doing here?"

"Came to fix the little lady's car. Give her what she needs. And you've already tied her hands. Nice. Ready for a little duck action."

CHAPTER SIXTEEN

"Take her to the old mine."

I looked at him, seeing for the first time the man who'd attacked me at the storage facility. He was taller than Scooter, probably six-two, with thick brown hair that fell into his eyes— eyes that glinted with drugs and malice, but were an amazing green that picked up the light on the mountain. He was broad shouldered, dressed in grease-stained jeans and a long-sleeved thermal t-shirt that showed incredible muscles. Tattoos in dark blue rose from the collar up his neck and along his jaw.

Scooter stepped back. Until this moment, Scooter had been the boss.

"Give her anything?" Carl—I knew he was Carl—asked. Scooter shook his head. "Why not?"

"No need," he rasped. "She's cooperating."

"With her hands tied," Carl laughed. "Some cooperation. You won't be running away this time, Scooter. You'll get to stay and watch. Learn something maybe."

He reached into his pocket, pulled out his phone. "No reception, still, on this side of the mountain. I can't believe they're still in the dark ages here. Down in SoCal, there's reception everywhere."

Scooter started to walk, with his hand on my arm, now rubbing it lightly, almost as if reassuring me.

"What's your name again?" Carl said.

"Sal."

"Sal, you should be thanking me."

"What for?"

"I saved your bacon, you know."

"No, I don't know."

"Scooter here, him of the angelic singing voice," Carl laughed, and Scooter's grip tightened on my arm, "he had the gossip columnist, my former partner, believe it or not—*thanks, Dad*—up here. Goddam thief. She was a little high, the buzz made her imagine there were bees in her blouse. So she tears her top off, and Scooter—you know what, Scooter? Maybe you like boys too, just like the mayor does, huh? Is that it? Big tits, red hair, gal tears her shirt off for you, and what do you do? Run like baby."

"Shut up, Carl," Scooter said.

"I had to finish the job for him," Carl said to me. "But I didn't really get to finish the job, no duck action, if you know what I mean. Broad falls down, breaks her leg. Scooter leaves her in the cave with a busted leg, she couldn't even run away, and he just bounds down the mountain like a deer."

Where had I heard that? From the laborer who came to see the Keeper. I should have told Devon. Did I? I was lightheaded with fear.

"Hey. You're not paying attention," Carl said. He smacked my behind, making me jump. "You're kind of spacey. And your car? You should take better care of it. A Prius should run forever. Except if you put air in the gas tank. Then it gets the hiccups until the electric motor takes over." He laughed an ugly little laugh.

We couldn't see the vineyards now that we were on the other side of Mount Santabella, away from Simpato. There were black holes in the side of the mountain, where the mines had been, and the trail had vestiges of double ruts where the carts must have run. I looked down at a stream flowing through the landscape, something I hadn't seen before, and a road that wound into the mountain. It had to be the back way, the way that connected to Peaches.

"Here's where you should have taken Georgiana, Scooter. Behind the mountain. Even with a broken leg she would have been numb for a while; you could have made her walk. She was still conscious when I got to her—man, I could have gotten some duck action. Some revenge for all the money she stole from me. No one would have found her for days. Instead Sal and who, Karen Monarch? Who calls herself Carinna now? You two found her in no time. Changed everything."

He stopped, turning toward a large, dark opening in the mountain. "Well, no one will find you for a while. Have a seat," he added.

With my hands tied, no longer with any feeling at all in them, it was hard to maneuver to the ground. I hit my knee as I went down and yelped.

"You can scream if you want," Carl said, almost kindly. "No one will hear you, and you might enjoy it." He pushed me back, and now I was lying on my hands. "Turn her over," he said. Scooter reached under me, and rolled me face down. "Now, for some duck action. Take notes, Scooter. You might learn something."

I was not going to let this happen to me. I lay very still, trying to figure out how to get out of this. Carl was jacked from working out in prison, obviously, and was clearly on drugs. Scooter, aggressive and volatile, was in some sort of thrall to Carl, the high-school hero. And I was somewhere unfamiliar on this god-forsaken mountain. What could I offer? Draft a free will and estate plan for them?

What did you offer a man who'd been so humiliated by his father that he'd killed him?

"Carl," I said. "Thank you."

"I like it," he said, "but what for? I haven't even ducked you yet." I could hear him moving behind me.

"You may not know it, but you saved a life."

He stopped.

"You were a kid, you know. You were young, and from what I heard, you were a pretty amazing athlete. Handsome, and I'm not flattering you, trust me, and well-liked by your classmates." I swallowed, face into the floor of the old abandoned mine. "My mom told me."

Even the movement of the air stopped. It was a huge gamble. Scooter moved slightly closer; I could see his boots.

"She said you were unjustly treated. That you were strong, and brave, and no young man should be treated the way you were. And yet, scared—" I needed another word, not *scared*—"determined as you were, you didn't let August take the rap for you. You knew he couldn't defend himself; you could have thrown him under the bus. But you didn't. And that saved his life."

I heard him sigh. And at that moment, Scooter lunged at him, and they both fell on top of me, knocking the air out of my lungs.

I saw black. I tried to get my breath. They were rolling off me, and despite my bound hands I was able to bend my knees enough to turn onto my side. I saw the flash of a knife, and with my last air, I screamed. Screamed as if my life depended on it. And then I thrust my legs into Carl, behind his knees.

He went down, and Scooter was on him. The knife flashed. "There! You won't talk either!" His knife went across Carl's throat, under his jaw, and blood spurted onto his shirt. And mine. And Scooter's.

Carl toppled forward.

Scooter turned to me. "I'll be back."

And like the other man had said, I watched Scooter bound, deer-like, down the mountain.

We lay on the hard ground in silence. "You knew," Carl

finally rasped. "You knew I killed him, but you understood why. No one else ever has."

Absolution. His father's death haunted him. As Scooter, or was it August, said, he was different. *Born that way,* with a shocking lack of empathy. But this was his father, who'd raised him alone, the only parent he ever knew. Maybe his father lacked empathy too, the essential humanity that would have spared his son such scarring public humiliation.

Absolution was false, he hadn't earned it and he didn't deserve it. And no one would absolve him for attacking Tilly's little cousin. Or sending that letter to my parents, the one that sent them on that deadly trip to Hawai'i. Or killing Georgiana. But for now, I could offer him words, the lawyer's stock in trade, to save my life.

"You're forgiven," I said. "You had to do it. He gave you no choice."

He closed his eyes. The bleeding had slowed. Scooter hadn't hit the big artery, it seemed, and if help arrived soon enough the cut wouldn't be fatal.

I heard voices and breathed a sigh of relief. Carl heard them too and started to try to get up. He wove and fell down again. He couldn't do it. Even with the drugs in his system, nothing could spur him to run once more.

And the most welcome sight on earth—Tilly, Devon, and August—filled the cave opening.

★ ★ ★

"I was driving by your house," August said, "and I saw Scooter and you. And you didn't look too good. I thought maybe you were sick, and he was taking you over to the hospital. But the truck was going the wrong way. So I went to turn around in your driveway, and who do I see gunning his truck backward, but Carl Montefusco. I couldn't believe it. I'd heard he was back, living in Cragstown, and that he'd learned how to be a mechanic in prison, but I didn't know what he was doing here in your driveway. With Scooter taking you somewhere, it was like the nightmare was all coming back. So I went to see Sergio. And that's when Tilly's call came in."

We were sitting at the police station, in the little interview room, August, Tilly, Devon, and I, with excellent coffee. Tilly patted my hand. "I was driving my traffic enforcement truck on Peaches, and I saw Scooter's truck parked wrong, at the vineyards, halfway up the curb and facing toward the mountain. I kept going, since I was trying to decide if I should give him a ticket or not, I mean, it's Scooter, right, when I saw another truck pull up behind it. He *also* parks up on the curb! I couldn't let *two* trucks park on the sidewalk like that. But before I could turn around, this guy who looked kind of familiar jumped out. And he started hustling right up the mountain. Not like a hiker, or a runner, but like someone who had business up there, and he knew where he was going. So I called Sergio to run the plates."

"It's a good thing you did," Devon said. "She doesn't have to call in the plates just to write a ticket," he added to me. "Good instincts."

"It just felt off," Tilly said. "As soon as I saw whose plates they were, I called the chief. While I was on the phone with the chief, August drove up and said he was worried, and wanted me and him to go up there, but Chief said to stay where we were."

"Sergio told me where Tilly was, just by the back of the mountain. Enough bad stuff had already gone down, I had to come anyway," August said. "I'd never forgive myself, if something happened to you. Your mom saved my life, you know."

"I know," I said.

I'd have to tell Devon all, but not with everyone there.

CHAPTER SEVENTEEN

My second week in Simpato started much like the first, with August blasting his horn as he went past my driveway, and Saul sending me angry emails demanding to know why I was still ignoring his texts. At noon my new phone arrived, and by one in the afternoon I was back in business. I'd lost everything that wasn't backed up to the cloud, but I would probably never miss whatever was gone. Unfortunately, Saul's number wasn't among the vanished.

At 1:05 I got a photo text from him. Luna the cat was front and center, with a smug look on her whiskery face. I sighed and punched in Saul's number.

"Finally!" he said.

"Hello," I suggested.

"Yeah, hello, Sal. What's the idea, ignoring me for a week?"

Where to start? I kept it simple. "I dropped my phone in the lake. I told you that in an email. There's no phone store here in Simpato, so I had to order a new one. It just arrived. Congratulations, you're caller number one."

"Funny funny."

"Well, I did get a burner phone—"

"What are you now, a drug dealer?"

I ignored the comment. "And I tried to call you, but you

didn't pick up. But never mind, Saul. What do you want?" It was his turn to be silent, an experience so rare that I panicked and listened for his breath. "Why so hostile?" he said, finally.

Um, because you cheated on me, lied to the State Bar, and got me suspended? "I hope you're not looking for a reconciliation, or to work together again," I said.

He laughed, but it rang hollow. "You need to take the goddam cat," he exhaled.

The cat? "I thought Melissa"—that was the intern—"wanted the cat."

More silence. "Just get the cat, okay?"

I smiled. Trouble in legally suspended paradise. "Okay, I'll get her this weekend. But that's it. We're divorced, remember?"

"Sal?" he said a bit plaintively.

I hung up. I lived in Simpato now.

★ ★ ★

That night, Devon knocked on the back door a little after eight. I let him in, poured some wine. "That was quite a day, yesterday," he said. "I'm glad it's over." He leaned back in his chair.

"Me too, but there are so many things I don't get. I still don't understand what the mayor's role was in all of this. Or how my car was involved."

"Long, long story. The mayor is basically a good guy. He and Georgiana were at odds for a decade, from the moment Giancarlo Montefusco made her an owner in Montefusco LLC. She was quite the manipulator and a great strategist. She was the one who handled all of the complicated stuff with the State, with the Environmental Protection Agency, the impact reports, in exchange for five percent of the ownership."

"I thought that the mayor and Montefusco were buddies and wanted the development to go through." I still wasn't completely sure what Devon knew about Montefusco's and Solis's activities at the monastery. I'd told him about the disaster with Carl and his friends that led to the murder, but since I hadn't been there, I had to tell it from Scooter's point of view. And he said the mayor was ineffectively trying to pull Montefusco off his son.

"That was then. Ten years ago. But after Montefusco was killed, Carl inherited. Apparently, the LLC paperwork . . ."

"Operating agreement," I supplied.

"Right, that left the dad's interest to Carl. There was some problem with him accessing it."

"Carl wasn't eighteen yet," I added, "so Georgiana—oh! Of course! She hid behind the name SansCanard, which is French for Without a Duck, by the way."

Devon chuckled. "Anatra is Italian for Duck."

"Jeez, the jokes just don't quit out here." It was my turn to explain things to Devon. "Anyway, Carl inherits ninety-five percent of Montefusco LLC, but SansCanard manages it. Scooter figures it out, and when Carl comes of age and needs money, Scooter helps him contact SansCanard. Carl sells bits and pieces of his interest in the vineyard for what seems like a lot of money to him, but is basically five cents on the dollar."

"Exactly. When, not *if,* when we find Scooter, we'll find out if he knew that SansCanard was the Nose."

"He must have figured it out; he's good at research. When Carl got out of jail last year, he thought he still had a good percentage of a vineyard property, valuable as it was, and worth a couple of million if it could be developed. And his father's old friend, the mayor, was opposing the development," I said.

"Once he got up here, he found out that Georgiana owned over ninety percent of *his* property, instead of him. She'd been screwing him over royally when he was young and vulnerable."

"Except," Devon said, "he'd also killed his father. So young and vulnerable, maybe, but also a murderer. And the people who knew that were August and Scooter, who didn't dare talk. It's likely that our friend the Nose figured it out, seeing how, well, nosy she was. But I think they're the only ones who really knew."

"My mom," I said softly.

"And your mom," he agreed.

"What will happen to Carl now? I asked.

"He's claiming that when he reached Georgiana, she was conscious, but her leg was broken. She got freaked—she was on meth—when she saw him, tried to get up and run, and fell and hit her head. That he never touched her. I don't know."

"And the rock just, what, jumped into my storage box? The horsehead in The Godfather, Simpato style? To warn me away?"

"Actually," Devon said, "that's a good analogy. I mean, he could have just thrown the rock down the mountain and no one would have ever found it."

"He couldn't have been thinking rationally at that instant when he bashed her head in. And when he realized he still was holding it, what better place to leave it than the Keeper's daughter's house? Let her know he was watching. And I think that's when he put air in my gas tank. Then, once he realized that August had moved the boxes, he knew he had to get the rock back. So he attacked me."

"Well, he'll definitely be charged with assault. Assault on you, on Tilly's cousin, and maybe Georgiana."

"God, that's depressing. He's going to get away with it," I said. "I can't ID him in the attack at the storage unit, there's no witnesses except Scooter to everything else. Unless the mayor comes forward and tells what happened ten years ago, I don't know how you'll get a conviction."

"We have time. We'll make it stick. It would help if the mayor would come clean. But there's a lot at stake for him."

"Where is he? I take it, since you're talking about him like that, that he's not dead on the mountain somewhere."

"Nah. Solis always lands on his feet, it seems. He and the

Cragstown mayor had just inked the deal they'd made with Pathways last Friday. He was going to announce it at the Little Sisters, but the Nose showed up at the service. That threw him. So he headed up to Cragstown. That's where he was hiding. He'd been driving up to tell the mayor, but Carl Montefusco had done something to his car, and when a coyote ran out of the hills he spun out."

"So Mayor Solis and the Cragstown mayor aren't lovers?"

Devon sighed. "Maybe they are. But that's not what was fueling the development. Georgiana was holding that over his head, threatening to out him in her column. Even though there aren't that many people, even in Simpato, who'd care anymore if he *is* gay, if it came out that he was in bed with the Cragstown mayor, and that's where the development was going, there would be hell to pay."

"Did you get the draft of Monday's column?" I asked.

He nodded. "We had to get a warrant. But yeah, and sure enough, there was the bit about Solis and Cragstown's mayor being *very good friends*. Not sure Edwina would have printed it if it had been any more specific. *And,* that Carl was back, and maybe an old Simpato mystery might finally be solved. That's what got her killed."

"Poor thing," I said, "her goose was cooked."

Devon rolled his eyes.

I got up and went into the kitchen. "More wine?" I poured us each another glass of the beautiful Simpato Vineyards Cabernet, and swirled it in our glasses.

"Oh my god! The glasses!" I dashed to the freezer. "Margo Schwartz!"

"Who?"

"Sister Marigold! Her real name is Margo Schwartz, and she says she's an investigative reporter. I think I just figured out what she's writing about!"

"Slow down. What?"

I handed him the tainted glasses, still wrapped in a nun's coif. "Long story." I told him about Margo, and Ginger, and Scooter. "All the more reason you've got to find Scooter. But Margo: I bet she's writing about Ephedra. If quote-Sister-unquote Ephedra laced the lemonade, I'll bet she's running some kind of drug ring out of the monastery! Never mind that she's got her investment fingers all over the town real estate!"

"You've been hiding this all week?" Devon was Chief again, pulling out his gloves to unwrap the glasses.

"No! This all happened yesterday."

Devon rubbed his face. "Your glasses, the ones that—I guess one of the nuns had left on your doorstep—they came back clean, by the way."

"I still don't know why I got them. Whether they were a tipoff, someone trying to tell me that the glasses were suspect, or the lemonade. Or someone trying to warn me—don't drink the lemonade. Another horsehead, or duck-head."

"No more wine for you, Sal," he smiled. "Maybe we should get some dinner."

I shrugged on my short leather jacket, grabbed my keys, and went to lock the door behind me. "No need," Devon said. "There's no crime in Simpato."

ABOUT THE AUTHOR

CLAUDIA H. LONG is the author of seven novels, including the brand-new small-town Duck series, as well as the deeply emotional mystery series featuring Zara and Lilly: *Nine Tenths of the Law* and *Our Lying Kin* (Kasva Press). Her books span centuries and topics, including Hidden Jews of Mexico during the Inquisition, women in the mining industry in 1753, women in the labor movement in 1920s San Francisco, and the legacy of inherited trauma. Her mysteries are also funny. When she isn't working as a lawyer or writing novels, she is a weaver, a passionate cook, and a grandmother.

Claudia H. Long

https://claudiahlong.com/

ACKNOWLEDGMENTS

With deepest gratitude, I would like to thank the city of Calistoga for the inspiration for this book. Everything that is good about Simpato is inspired by my lovely new hometown. Everything that isn't good about Simpato is the product of my overactive imagination. And of course, no person, living or dead, is portrayed in this story.

Thank you to Julia Park Tracey and Vicki DeArmon for choosing *Murder without a Duck* for their exclusive line of Sibylline Digital First books, and to Maureen Jennings for her thoughtful and thorough editing.

Thank you to my agent, April Eberhardt, for her encouragement and support; to Denise Steele for reading an early version of the novel; and to Paul Ingalls for his advice on the issues facing small-town newspapers, along with the proper roles of editors. Any errors are mine, I assure you!

Thank you to my adult children, Julia and Will, who eagerly await the next book.

And most of all, thank you to Clyde. You make it all possible.

Calistoga, California, 2024

BOOK CLUB QUESTIONS

1. Sal moves from San Francisco to the small town of Simpato while she recovers from a divorce and a suspension of her law license. Many books start with the premise of a woman seeking emotional shelter in a small town during a personal crisis. Do you think that moving is a good response to crisis? What does this trope provide for the theme of the novel?

2. How does the small-town vibe help her recover her equanimity—or does it? Everyone seems to know her business. Does that help her? How would you react to being recognized at the grocery store and the café when you have suffered an embarrassing personal setback?

3. Scooter can't shake his high-school nickname, or his past. Have you known people who remain attached to their high-school identities long past graduation? How has Scooter's past held him back? Why is he still in thrall to Carl?

4. Carl is another character who can't shake an early trauma. How has the past shaped him? How is his trauma different from Scooter's and August's?

5. Sal's parents' fate remains a mystery at the end of the book. Do you think they were forced out of Simpato? Do you think Sal will try to find out more now that she's returned to the town?

6. Newspapers are struggling for readers, and small-town papers barely exist anymore. How are they important to the life of the town? Have they been replaced by message boards and social media? What's lost, and what's gained?